LAST STAND!

On all sides, hooves pounded the sandy soil as Major Cavanaugh led his cavalrymen into the encampment. Bullets whizzed like angry bees, riddling the hide lodges.

Warriors fired from behind trees and boulders, while others raced around on horseback with rifles and lances.

Up and down the lines, the pony soldiers made their shots count. As they dealt death, Comanche bullets sang back.

The camp looked like a slaughterhouse, the ground splashed with blood and littered with dead cavalrymen and Indians. Still, the battle-crazed Comanches fought on. They charged at the weakened flank of the soldiers' main force in a densely massed wave, dozens deep.

Sergeant Keogh galloped close to Marcus. "Back off, Major! For God's sake, back off! Here they come!"

"Back off, hell! If we break this last charge, they're whipped!" Marcus flourished his pistol and took the lead. "At 'em, men! Give 'em hell!"

Other books in the **ARROW AND SABER** series:

COMANCHE WAR

G.A. CARRINGTON

A DELL BOOK

For Marilyn

Special thanks to Charley W. Perlberg

Published by
Dell Publishing
a division of Bantam Doubleday Dell
Publishing Group, Inc.
666 Fifth Avenue
New York, New York 10103

ISBN: 0-440-20382-1

Printed in the United States of America
Published simultaneously in Canada

February 1990

10 9 8 7 6 5 4 3 2 1

OPM

Chapter One

Fierce, sharp pain jolted Lieutenant Hayes Bingham's right elbow. The young officer's good hand clutched his arm where the Comanche arrow had struck. His uniform sleeve was slick with blood around the feathered shaft. Wounded at the worst of times, when the few folks left alive on the besieged emigrant train needed him most! By an act of will, he fought back the pain and kept his position, but try as he might, he couldn't lift or fire his service revolver with the injured arm.

The acrid smell of gunpowder drifted in the prairie wind and mingled with smoke from blazing wagon bonnets. The Conestogas had been drawn into a circle, and several dozen dead defenders sprawled around its perimeter. The bulky draft horses, which had been hastily unhitched, were rearing and plunging in the improvised rope pen. On both sides of the officer, men and women knelt under wagon beds, firing rifles as fast as they could.

The redskins raced past on their paint-daubed ponies, slung low over the mounts' off flanks for cover and shooting under their animals' necks. The warriors' war cries rose above the noise of the crackling flames. Hoofbeats drummed, and the rattle of shots went on without letup.

A painted devil with a quill chest plate broke from the circling party, then steered his mount toward the gap between the wagons where Bingham stood, venting shrill *ki-yis*. As he closed in, he leveled an iron-tipped lance. Bingham used both hands to raise his heavy Schofield sidearm. He pulled the trigger. The Indian pitched backward and the riderless pony abruptly veered aside.

Before he could even feel his victory, a bullet punched the officer in the thigh, throwing his legs out from under him. He crashed down hard in the brittle summer grass. The Texas panhandle was a long way from Connecticut and his gracious family home. When he'd first been posted at the edge of the Staked Plains after West Point, Lieutenant Bingham had called the parched, forbidding flatland hell.

Now he found it hell indeed. Several more warriors had broken from their line to gallop close, shooting and yelling like fury. The lieutenant scrambled along the ground like an injured crawfish, the agony from his wounds racking him. Desperately, he tried to make it to the cover of a wagon off to his left, the one that belonged to Clementine's father and brother, Seth. Clementine, the woman he'd followed the wagon train in hopes of seeing again.

A mighty thunder of unshod hooves boiled close. Bingham rolled on his back, cocked his gun and fired. A stocky, muscled Indian dropped his war club and pitched from his mount's back. Another savage raider broke past the wagons, his pony rearing above the downed officer. This time the Schofield's hammer fell on an empty chamber. Hayes Bingham prepared to die.

Then another sound rang out, a fusillade directed from within the wagon circle. As Bingham stared, Clementine sped across the ground, firing and cocking a Winchester as fast as she could — and her slugs slammed home. The redskin who was menacing Bingham toppled. Several more who'd participated in the charge wheeled their animals in retreat.

The feisty young woman was at the lieutenant's side. "Hayes! Hayes! Hurry and run with me! Over by Pa and Seth at the wagon."

"I'm hit in the leg, Clemmy."

"Tarnation! Then get up and lean on me! Hurry! The redskins are riding on back this way!"

"I can't!"

"You've got to!" With that, she heaved him up with surprising strength. Half running, half dragging the hobbling man, she led him toward the cover of the wagon wheel. The Drury menfolk stretched flat on the ground under the wagon, firing occasionally at the raiding Indians. Bingham sensed they were low on ammunition. Dwight Drury, the older man, grimaced at each Indian he brought down at long range. Seth, a boy in his teens, just kept firing impassively.

The Comanches had broken their line again to charge. As the pony-riding hoard spread out abreast, the warriors who possessed guns used them, while the rest launched a rain of arrows. One pierced Dwight's neck. The old man reared up, gasped and collapsed, dead. Seth, seething with rage, rose and ran at the enemy on foot. He was cut down before he'd gone three steps.

Clementine kept her head and used her rifle the way her father had taught her. Kneeling in her skirts, she downed one brave while the wounded officer shot a second who rode in so close he fell within arm's reach. Then the woman was slammed by the impact of a .44-40 round. She spun backward, away from the wheel, and flopped beside the officer. Two-thirds of her face was torn away by the bullet, leaving a hideous crimson mash. Her gingham frock and Bingham's uniform were splashed with blood.

Along the ring of burning wagons, resisting gunfire ceased. Men, women and children lay in motionless heaps — all dead. Panic clutched Hayes Bingham. If he couldn't run without aid, he could crawl. With his brass buttons combing grass, he desperately sought a hiding place.

Behind him, ponies galloped up and the warriors who rode them shouted with savage rage. Then he heard a new sound cut the air, high and thin, distant but growing closer at the speed of a racing horse. It was an army bugle, frantically blowing the charge. Heavy gunfire followed it. The United States Cavalry was on its way!

"Fire at will, men! Damned red rascals! Kill all of 'em ye can!" Hayes Bingham heard the faint shout of a commanding officer. The wounded man's brain swam and he fainted from loss of blood.

Chapter Two

The wide lines of cavalry galloped across the hilly terrain toward the burning wagon train. Major Marcus Anthony Cavanaugh, the commander of C, D and F Companies on a march west from Fort Sill, rode in the center of the charge. To his left, a guidon-carrying corporal spurred his mount, and to his right, the trumpeter blasted his brass horn for all he was worth. Directly ahead stood the ring of wagons, most of them aflame. The attacking Comanches turned their attention from their emigrant prey, and wheeled their ponies about to confront the new threat.

Cavanaugh listened for shouts and renewed firing from the settlers with the train, hoping they were in time to save some lives. He lifted a gauntleted hand.

Sergeant Keogh's voice rang out. "Open fire!"

An early scattering of shots from the troopers turned into a deadly volley. Feather-bonneted Indians pitched backward from their mounts' backs.

They were clearly outnumbered, and this time by a well-armed force led by a seasoned officer. Marcus signaled again, and the troopers fanned out wider, riding hard to keep the hostiles from an easy retreat. The crack of dozens of army Springfields made an ominous rattle, their smoke forming a line of tiny white clouds under the bright sky.

At the urging of a bold war chief, the Comanche band rallied. As the soldiers rode into bow range, arrows flew in earnest, and with them came casualties. Before Marcus's eyes, a dragoon's blue uniform was pierced, the rigid shaft protruding from the man's chest. He somersaulted backward off his mount and was trampled by the horse coming up behind him. Another soldier was lifted from his McClellan saddle by a hurled lance. Marcus Cavanaugh's campaign hat gained a bullet hole.

Still, the cavalry rode onward.

Abruptly, the resistance stopped. One moment the opposing groups of riders were about to meet and clash. Suddenly, the Indians took to their heels, urging their ponies away to avoid being boxed in by the troopers on the flank. Marcus tossed several shots with his Colt, but already his targets had departed from range, jinking frantically from side to side.

There was a brief skirmish beyond the bunched wagons. Riding hard toward it, Marcus was forced to watch from afar. Aghast, he saw Corporal Henley's troop fall inexplicably back. The savages broke through into open prairie.

A few seconds later, the redskins split into dozens of groups of two or three riders and disappeared beyond the rolling hummocks of the terrain, abandoning their dead. Marcus Cavanaugh cursed quietly. His was an untried, newly formed command, but he thought the veterans, at least, would fight strongly if called upon. He'd been wrong.

The only thing left to do was to ride in and view the emigrants' situation. The sky-high billows of smoke that had drawn the cavalry to the scene had diminished, since the burning wagons were mostly consumed and caved in.

Still young in years for his rank, the trials of command had taken their toll on Major Marcus Cavanaugh's weathered face. Under his campaign hat, his forehead was scored and his hair had gray streaks about the temples. His carefully trimmed mustache was a salt-and-pepper blend of brown and gray. When his lieutenants came up beside him to receive directions, he barked out orders with his mouth set in a hard, straight line.

"Lieutenant Ambrose, deploy some lookouts to make sure the hostiles don't return. And have the recall sounded. Lieutenant Hazelcrest, see to accounting for our wounded and dead. The surgeon's already busy in the field, I see. Have him report inside the wagons' perimeter as soon as possible. There may be settlers in need of attention, too. Captain Turnbo and Sergeant Keogh, call some troopers along, and we'll ride on in." Under his breath, he cursed. "There are bound to be women and children killed by the savages. Damn!"

He urged his lathered black mount ahead, though it balked and grew skittish at the heavy scent of death. The party rode past damaged wheels and charred wagon tongues, their horses quivering and dancing nervously. High in the sky, the buzzards gathered, drifting lower and lower.

7

The carnage was terrible. The downed and thrashing horses in the rope pen were the least part of it. Marcus saw Keogh motion to some privates to put the animals out of their misery. Every person who had been with the wagon train, it seemed, had met the same fate already. The heaped corpses made a ghastly sight.

Marcus stepped from the saddle. At his feet, two children lay shot, their clothes dyed red with gore. The major's ice-blue eyes blinked briefly. A pregnant woman had caught an arrow in her belly and died. Several older females had been killed with bullets, and another's skull looked cleft with a hatchet.

Every male corpse held a gun in a stiffening grip, but there the similarity among them ended. Some were sprawled grotesquely on their backs, others lay face down. Still more had curled up tightly, clutching their wounds in fatal agony. Entrails had been blown from abdomens by .45-caliber rounds. Heads were pierced by slugs. One peaceful-looking gent had a clean, gaping hole above one eye. Most defenders had sustained arrow wounds, and some of them resembled pincushions.

"Major! You'd best come here and take a look!" The voice belonged to the swarthy scout, Sabine Gilliam, a half-white, half-Delaware tribesman from the Indian Territory. Somehow he'd come to be called by the name of the Texas river. Now his dark eyes flashed across the space of the circled wagons at Marcus Cavanaugh.

The major strode toward Gilliam. He passed a lowly recruit private who was puking his guts out beside the body of a woman without a face. The major grimly noted the burnished-golden hair.

"For God's sake, be a man, Private! Pull yourself together!"

"Y-yes sir!" The kid looked barely better after his commander's stern words. Marcus stepped past him and stood beside the buckskin-clad scout.

"A survivor of the raid, then!" He took in the form of a man in a blue uniform stretched out in the wagon's shade, his chest heaving with labored breaths. "A cavalryman shot here, inside the circle! And an officer! Not one of ours?"

"Oh, you're going to recognize him, sir, when I crouch down and turn his head your way. Just watch." Gilliam knelt, cradled Hayes Bingham's shoulders in his wiry arms and lifted the injured man. He was careful not to touch the protruding arrow.

"I see what you mean. It's Bingham, the man we sent ahead to occupy the cantonment till we arrived and made preliminary preparations."

"So's he'd be able to tell us how the land lay with the Comanches."

"Now he's told us. More than we anticipated."

Captain Phil Turnbo came up and stood at Marcus's shoulder. His features were frozen in a mask. "Major Pike the surgeon is on his way. It'll be hell to pay if the boy dies, won't it, Major Cavanaugh?"

Marcus shrugged. "That depends on his father, General Bingham."

Brigadier General Cyrus Bingham normally worked at the department headquarters in San Antonio, but the reins that this military leader held reached far. One of the facts known throughout the division of the Missouri, of which Texas was a part, concerned the the general and his son. The general wanted great things for the boy.

Lieutenant Hayes Bingham was under Marcus Cavanaugh's direct command, but at the moment, wounded and dying at a place where he didn't belong. Only if he regained consciousness could he explain.

The surgeon, a big man with a walrus-sized mustache, bustled up with his kit. His tunic sleeves were rolled high, his hands, wrists and clothing stained with blood. He knelt by Hayes Bingham's pale form.

"Will he regain consciousness?"

"We can always hope, Major. Let me examine the boy. I'll be a few minutes. Nothing you can do to help, so if you have anything else that needs attending. . . ."

Marcus ordered Sergeant Keogh to put burial details to work. He stood silently with Captain Turnbo and waited. Finally, the surgeon motioned them over.

"Well?"

"It's a hard choice. An arm bone and a leg bone, both of them badly shattered."

"For God's sake, man, out with it!" Turnbo snapped.

"I'm going to have to amputate."

The United States Army provided its medical men with superb tools. A seventeen-by-four-by-seven-inch field-surgery kit bound in leather held an array of instruments, from scalpels to skull-piercing trepans and a sturdy bone saw of Toledo steel. The trouble with battleground amputations was the poor conditions. Major Pike had a supply of laudanum to kill the pain, but not a generous supply. And he would do his sterilizing with searing heat and boiling water.

He set a couple of enlisted men to kindling a roaring blaze. They found a barrel in one of the wagons that they tapped for water. By the time steam was pumping from the large kettle — also found among emigrant effects — Pike had his patient stretched out on a ground blanket. Four burly privates gathered to perform holding chores. Scalpels and saw were laid out, ready for Pike's hand. Unluckily, the patient came awake before he could begin, moaning his pain. Young Bingham tried to sit up, but fell back from weakness. But by then, Marcus had seen the effort and approached.

"Major Cavanaugh?" the wounded man said weakly through half-closed eyes, seeing his commanding officer materialize overhead.

"Don't try to salute, Lieutenant, considering how you're hurt. We're planning on good Doc Pike here pulling you through, you know."

The shavetail groaned anew. "Never should've ridden out to the wagons from the post alone . . . Clementine . . . by God, she was a beauty! Savages killed her." Sweat stood out like bullets across his forehead, and his sandy hair was dark with it. Then, abruptly, a look of fear clouded his youthful features. "The general, he doesn't need to hear about this escapade, sir! There'll only be a scar or two from my wounds."

The enlisted men's eyes studied their boots. Marcus knelt beside Hayes Bingham. "Your father, the general, he has ways of finding out most things that go on in this man's army."

The lieutenant glanced about him, vaguely noticing the blue summer sky, the unburned wagon that loomed overhead, shading him. He seemed to notice for the first time that he'd been stripped of his blouse and trousers. Then his feverish gaze took in the array of instruments. His face was stricken with horror.

"The liquid in the brown bottle is laudanum, son," Doc Pike told him gently. "It'll help you forget the pain. Swallow this spoonful or I'll have to force it down your throat."

"You're not going to butcher off my limbs, Christ, no! I'd rather die. Christ, Pike, just kill me, won't you! Instead of . . . instead of . . . !"

The surgeon gestured. The four enlisted men closed in, grabbing the patient, pinning him to the ground.

"No!" Bingham roared. "No!"

Marcus turned away.

"Major?" Keogh had come quietly up to him.

"What is it, Sergeant?"

"Gilliam, sir. He's been out examinin' the Injun dead. He's found somethin' he says he wants ye to see."

"I'll come right now."

A final scream broke from Lieutenant Bingham's lips. Pike's scalpel bit deep into the flesh of the shattered arm above the shaft of the arrow. Bingham fell back, mercifully fainting from shock.

As Marcus and Keogh strode away, they heard the monotonous rasp of Pike's saw stroking the young man's bone.

It had been a grueling march of many days, west out of Fort Sill, their ultimate destination the small outpost called the Cantonment on the Sweetwater. The mission was to reoccupy the place, now abandoned for a little more than a year. The War Department's divisional headquarters in Chicago had the idea of protecting the growing number of cattle drives to the Kansas railheads. The Comanche and Kiowa nations had been forced onto reservations. Most had submitted. But not all.

Major Marcus Cavanaugh, like every man-jack in the column, was butt sore and bone weary, and after the hectic afternoon action against the raiding party, his body cried out for rest. Nonetheless, he hiked without complaint beside the beefy Irish sergeant.

Just outside the ring of the ruined emigrants' wagons, Keogh paused. "There the chief scout is a-squattin' in the buffalo grass, sir. He's gathered himself quite a pile of guns off the dead red devils."

Marcus saw what the noncom meant and his attention was sparked. It wasn't a single pile of firearms he found himself looking at as he approached Sabine Gilliam, but two. The smaller consisted of three older rifles and six-guns, the kind of junk the plains tribes ordinarily carried.

The other pile, larger by far, contained almost-new Winchester repeating carbines, gleaming from the animal fat smeared to keep them rust-free. There was no question that they had been in the Indians' hands when they attacked the train. There were feathers tied onto them, and the walnut stocks had been decorated with carvings and paint. Marcus recognized the manufacturer's latest model, a very efficient weapon indeed against the army's .50-caliber single-shots — charcoal-furnaces as the men called them.

The major emitted a low whistle. "An interesting

haul, Gilliam. Very interesting."

Usually the scout's face was an unreadable slate, but now his anger showed through. "They had to've been sold to the Comanches by white men, and right out of the factory boxes, sir. If they'd been taken off settlers or drivers or such, they wouldn't all be the same kind. Plus there'd be signs of wear on the guns."

"Things look bad for keeping the wild tribes off the war path if this is going on." Marcus stroked his lean jaw. "We're lucky the entire band didn't have the new rifles. A lot of bows and arrows are still being used. Otherwise, they'd have made it worse for us."

"Aye," Sergeant Keogh muttered worriedly.

"Shall I have these hauled along to the post we're headin' for, Major?" Sabine Gilliam wanted to know. "Clean 'em up, ready 'em for our own use?"

"That's not the way the army works. The guns aren't standard issue. But yes, throw them on one of the wagons that survived burning. We'll be taking along the lot, including furniture and any supplies. If any next of kin show up to make claim, fine. If not, officers' quarters always needs beds and chairs. Which reminds me, Sergeant Keogh."

"Yes sir?"

"Have a bed made ready in a wagon for transporting casualties who can't ride. I'm thinking mainly of Lieutenant Bingham. We'll bivouac here tonight, and push on at first daylight. We should make the Cantonment on the Sweetwater tomorrow."

"By all the saints! I forgot about the lieutenant! You reckon he's survived havin' his arm and leg cut off?"

A shriek of agony reached them on the hot plains wind.

14

Cavanaugh glanced quickly in that direction and turned back to Keogh. "He's made it until now, Sergeant. We'll go on hoping for the best."

Chapter Three

Cantonment on the Sweetwater was an outpost of Fort Sill, that was built to prevent re-entry of reservation tribes from Indian Territory into west Texas. Located near the headwaters of Sweetwater Creek, a tributary of the North Fork of the Red, the place had water throughout the year, though it was muddy for drinking during the dry months. The weather was typically panhandle, broiling in summer, in winter, subject to quixotic blizzards and cold. And almost without letup, the strong, dusty wind blew long and hard.

Major Cavanaugh caught sight of the small outpost when he was still far away. The clutch of structures baked in the dazzling midday sun, and floating just beyond a curtain of distorting heat waves. The spirits of the troops and officers lifted at the prospect of bunks and roofs over their heads, not to mention better food. They'd emerged from hilly terrain miles back, but still had quite a distance across the plain to cross.

The flatland was broken only by faint traces of old buffalo trails, patches of hard ground where the grass found it difficult to grow. These were left from when herds ranged fifty miles in length, and took days to cross one's path. A time less than five years past, but gone forever.

"I remember the buffler, all right," Sabine Gilliam was telling Marcus. The scout rode his shaggy dun close to the commander's black, but a two-pace lag behind, as proper respect dictated. "They made a powerful sight. And fed a powerful plenty of red people. The white hunters took 'em just for their hides, of course, leavin' carcasses to rot. And then one day there was just this big plain full of bones. Next thing, bone pickers was comin' along in raggedy carts to gather 'em. They claimed bones was needed back east to make china plates."

"And cups and saucers, Gilliam." Marcus's custom was to let the scout ramble on whenever he would. Most days he was far from talkative, a trait of his mixed-blood heritage, Marcus supposed. No one knew how old the half-Delaware was, but his copper features were unwrinkled. His crankiness couldn't relate to old age.

One thing could always be counted on, however. He was the best reader of trail signs the command had seen. The man was dependable in the way it was most important — in the matter of his job.

Marcus changed the subject from the buffalo days. "We'll be at the cantonment well before sundown, I suppose."

"Unless we give the horses their heads and let 'em drink in the stream that winds close to our road ahead. See the good green grass layin' by the water?

17

If we don't want sluggish mounts, we'll have to keep 'em back from there. Especially them as pulls the wagons."

Marcus glanced behind him at the column. Several of the wagons that had belonged to the slain emigrants, driven now by troopers, brought up the rear. A single Conestoga, carrying those wounded in the previous day's fight with the Comanches, came on the leaders' heels. This was a thoughtful move that relieved them from breathing the dust raised by ninety mounted soldiers. The only problem with the arrangement resulted from groans. Marcus had been forced to listen to them for mile after mile. Now he heard a particularly shrill one. It was Bingham.

"Well, it won't be long now, Sergeant," the major told Keogh, leaning in his saddle toward the noncom.

"No, it won't, sir, saints be praised."

The wagon jolted in a rut and Hayes Bingham screamed again. Marcus faced the broiling, westward-leaning sun, and trotted on without pause.

Cavanaugh stood with Captain Turnbo in front of the headquarters building. The troopers of the companies had packed their equipment in, and the parade was empty. The eyes of both officers scanned the post.

"Think it'll take long to whip the men and this godforsaken place in shape?"

"We aren't going to let it take long."

The smoke from the officers' pipes blended as the pumpkin-colored sun slid down the sky. The stiff, dry wind that had blown all day had turned to vagrant light breeze, and the view, as long as one focused afar, was not particularly unpleasant. Closer at hand, though, the vantage point commanded an array of structures that had suffered nearly a year of neglect. With the reopening of the Cantonment on the Sweetwater, Marcus saw, the first job of the commander was going to be to order substantial repairs and carpentry.

Like many other army outposts on the arid Western frontier, this one was constructed of sod blocks. There was the usual scattering of storage sheds, farriers' barns, a hospital, latrines, but among these loomed three main buildings, larger and more elaborate: an enlisted men's barracks, officers' quarters and the sprawling headquarters containing an orderly room and offices. Despite a scarcity of indoor space, military policy was followed as to eating accommodations. Separate mess halls for officers and noncoms were each housed in different structures. There was a broad parade ground for conducting drills, and beyond it, the paddock.

"Reckon the strikers have got our sleeping rooms ready?" Turnbo, done with smoking, rapped his pipe against the base of the flag staff.

"They're good enough at the servanting type of chore. I'm supposing the rooms are fit to clean up and shave in. And I intend to before supper, Captain."

"Don't we all?"

The two officers were joined by a third, younger and without the older men's hard, hollow-eyed appearance. First Lieutenant Nathan Ambrose had been tested in battle against the Cheyennes under Custer in the Black Hills mission, but his raw exuberance hadn't yet been tarnished.

Just give it time, Marcus Cavanaugh mused, as the three struck off across the yard. Aloud, he said, "If the

Comanche would only allow things to stay as peaceful as they look just now. That's not likely, though, what with whites now selling guns to Leaping Wolf. That trade is certain to send north Texas up in a flaming Indian war. Just a matter of time."

"Sabine Gilliam believes the chief troublemaker is this Leaping Wolf?" Ambrose had first heard of the war leader back at Sill. The brave had a reputation as a wily and treacherous antagonist, and warriors flocked to him. In addition, the tribesmen he led had been called the finest light cavalry in the world. But the young officer had yet to see this firsthand. Surely the better-mounted, better-armed United States Army would be able to defeat the foe. And yet, if the Comanches had access to repeaters and became formidably armed, it might be a different story.

"By all accounts of those who've fought him," Marcus replied, "Leaping Wolf is as good a tactician as Quanah Parker ever was, but without that chief's regard for his people's future."

"When Quanah's force got licked by MacKenzie, he let his Kwahadies be put on a reservation," Ambrose said.

"That's not quite true, Nate," Turnbo corrected. "Quanah's own band was never decisively defeated. The chief simply saw the writing on the wall. Took his people and all their animals into the fort. Told MacKenzie that he expected the white men to keep their word and see that everyone stayed fed. The first thing the colonel did was have the soldiers slaughter fifteen hundred horses belonging to the Indians — so there'd be no more roaming. Even that, Quanah endured. He didn't want to see his tribe wiped out."

"The point is," Marcus put in, "Leaping Wolf isn't

the type to surrender. Give him guns, and he'll keep battling to the last man. And nowadays it seems he's getting those guns!"

"Well, it'll have to stop." Nate Ambrose sniffed indignantly. "If need be, the government can send a whole regiment out here."

"The government doesn't think it can afford that many men to protect a route for cattle herds. That's why we're not big enough to be called Fort Something-or-other. A fort's home to a regiment. What's wanted here now is a small cantonment with a few companies of cavalry."

"But if we're overrun — "

"That's a threat we have to face."

The officers at Sweetwater were far from cheerful, even by day, and the onrush of dusk had engulfed the area with dismal shadows. An outbreak of shouts up the lane in front of commissary stores drew them before they reached their cabins. All three pumped their legs into a run and rounded a corner to see a fight in progress. A trooper as scrawny as a beanpole brandished his fists, while a second private — this one burly and squat — watched for his opponent to drop his guard.

"Atten-*shun!*" barked one of several onlooking troopers.

"What's going on here?" Marcus snapped.

The arrival of the officers was ignored by the brawlers, who at that moment ran at each other with arms flailing and mouths spouting curses.

"Goddamn shit-kicker!" the huskier one growled, launching a roundhouse punch that grazed the skinny man's chin.

"Won't put up with no more raggin'," yelled Beanpole. "Take this, you bastard!" The man's long arm outreached his antagonist's and connected with the fellow's chest.

"Atta way, Kendall!" someone encouraged. "Orly deserves to get his ornery ass whupped!"

The man called Orly reacted as if hurt, stepping back and gusting a breath. Kendall kicked out with a booted foot, aiming at Orly's groin. But Cobb Orly had been faking. Quick as a peeved rattlesnake he threw himself to the side and let the foot hammer air. Swooping around and low, he came up from the ground with a scything uppercut. The blow connected with Kendall's lean jaw and the thin man was flung into a sod wall with a jarring thud. There were gasps from the onlookers as blood sprayed from the victim's split lip. Kendall dropped to the earth, rolling. His hand clawed at a stone the size of a small cabbage.

Marcus saw the way the fray was going. The fury in the combatants' eyes went deep and shouted commands weren't likely to be obeyed. The squat one looked mean and stupid by nature, and his attacker was goaded into mindless rage. In the next instant, the skinny Kendall hurled his rock from his position on the ground, but missed his target. Orly powered a heel to the downed man's ribs, drawing a howl of pain.

Sergeant Keogh and a couple of corporals ran up, but instead of charging directly in to overwhelm the brawlers, they paused to study their best move. Marcus decided to end it. Whipping his regulation army Colt from its holster, he fired into the air. At the bolt of sound and the spear of flame that cut the twilight, everyone froze.

22

A second later, Corporals Malthus and O'Reilly dove at Orly, clubbing him to the ground with bunched knuckles. Next, Malthus dipped to wrap a hand in Kendall's hair, dragging him erect. Both battlers, with faces cut and bruised, were pushed to the storehouse wall. Their shirts were torn and filthy. They were puffing like locomotives and their eyes smoldered.

"March these boyos to the yard outside the smithy." Keogh grunted. "Since there's no guardhouse on the post as yet, we'll just have leg irons clamped to anchor 'em to a couple of anvils. When they cool off, their real punishment'll be decided."

Kendall and Orly were being hustled away when Marcus spoke. "Hold on just a minute. I'm curious. What was the cause of the fight?" Among the troopers who'd gathered, there was shuffling and muttering, but nobody spoke up. "None of the witnesses know? Then let the pair talk for themselves. Kendall, what about it? You're one cavalryman out of the three companies here, but I seem to recall your face. You been in trouble before?"

"Since joinin' the army, or in my life? Ain't been a sojer but a few months."

Keogh poked the man in the ribs. "Look at the major when you're talkin' to him. Do it for any and all officers yer in front of. And don't forget to call 'em *sir!*"

"Let him talk, Sergeant."

"Right, Major. I will."

The miserable military specimen spat pink phlegm, then started to talk with a heavy drawl of the eastern South. Mississippi, Marcus was inclined to judge, or maybe Tennessee.

"Awright, I signed up fer the army 'cause it had to be better'n paw's farm in them goddamn Tennessee hills! At least, so I reckoned, I'd be gettin' fed reg'lar. But I didn't count on polecats like that 'un figurin' they rule the roost!" His hand, plowhandle-calloused and scarred, pointed at Cobb Orly.

"Aw," Orly retorted, "he's a no-account son of a bitch!"

"Quiet!" Keogh roared. "Major, Orly's in his third enlistment, but a worse soldier I never did see. Gets mean drunk every payday. Loafs on fatigue details. After all these years, the man still can't drill! When he came to this new command, I got the word from other noncoms at Sill. They like him for only one thing: He hates redskins, and in a fight against 'em, he can be a terror."

"Is that so?" Marcus's features were washed in lamplight from the commissary store window. He appeared stern. "So it's the old story? Making the recruit's life miserable? That's the noncom's role, soldier," he said to Orly. "After this, do you think you can get along with Kendall?"

"If he shows proper respect."

"Major," Kendall burst out, "he tried to make me buy his soap dish carved from an Injun's head bone! I didn't want it, but he said he needed the money ta buy him a jug!"

"True?"

Orly shrugged.

"And he's got him a squaw-skin hatband — with hair — which he tried to make me sniff!"

Marcus registered distaste. "Not regulation, but I know plenty of troopers sport such throughout the army. I may not approve of Orly, Kendall, but I won't

24

tolerate fighting between the men under me. I'm going to inflict punishment on you both the same. Punishment you may find hard."

"What might it be?"

"You'll find out in the morning. March them away, Sergeant." Keogh saluted, and under the eyes of the other men, drove the culprits off on the double.

Across the outpost, a bugle's notes rang. Evening mess.

"Now for fresh game that the company hunters shot, and boiled beans." Phil Turnbo grinned at the other officers.

"What do you make of the antagonism among the men, Major?" Ambrose asked. "I get the impression that it's widespread."

Marcus nodded. "You're not wrong. This command was put together in a hurry, and we got the castoffs from a number of regiments. About half new enlistees, half experienced soldiers and just about all of them the army's dregs. Lazy. Inclined to disobey. A good many of those men have to be wanted for crimes someplace or other. We'll need discipline to make them into a decent combat force."

"And without driving them to desertion."

"There'll always be men deserting from these tougher posts. Our job is to mete out discipline tough, but fair, and that way keep the numbers down." Marcus was leading the way to the officers' mess.

First Lieutenant Nathan Ambrose wagged his head. "We have our work cut out. Our own men and those hostiles with their new repeating rifles."

"That, too," Marcus agreed. "But right now let's dig into roast antelope haunch."

Chapter Four

The work of repairing the outpost began immediately. Many of the sod buildings had crumbling roofs. Most of the walls, thanks to scant rainfall, were intact, but the holes tunneled by snakes and mice needed plugging, and badly, for they also admitted fleas, spiders and centipedes that kept troopers and officers hopping through the nights.

Crews of troopers sweated with spades and axes along the banks of the creek to dig clay and cut willow poles. Wagons were pressed into use for hauling, making dozens of round trips per day. For the task of roofing, poles were laid on crosspieces, clay was applied and topped off with a final dressing of sod, grass side up. The result wouldn't keep out hard, season-long rains, but then, there were none in the Texas panhandle. The men did what worked.

Progress was steady. Since there was need for more sheds and corrals, Marcus directed that fresh sod be taken from the prairie out beyond the compounds' perimeter. Several acres were stripped, slowly but surely, and the result was ugly, but there was no other way. Transporting lumber from places where timber grew was impractical and expensive.

So, for the first weeks that the outpost was occupied again, the men of the companies grew blisters on their hands, not their rumps. In view of these priorities, Marcus curtailed mounted and dismounted drills. The normal soldiering routines would be reinstated when the laboring squads completed jobs. Yet, both day and night around the clock, sentries were posted on sharp watch for Comanches. And scout parties ranged from the cantonment on horseback, scouring after signs of lurking warriors. There was no attack. Marcus got in the habit of thanking their lucky stars.

Hot, dry early summer turned to hot, dry midsummer, while the sun pounded the land like a flatiron. The flow of the Sweetwater gradually shrank, leaving broad banks of cracked, baked mud. The sky stayed bright and cloudless, looking down on horizons that shimmered. Buffalo grass turned brittle brown. Wind-witches danced erratically across the gaunt flat. When the sun was at its zenith, both men and horses wilted, but endured. The soldiers' skins, where exposed, became brown as old saddles.

On the first morning of July, Major Marcus Cavanaugh stalked the footpath from the headquarters to the hospital. Word had come by way of an orderly that Hayes Bingham had taken a turn for the better. The major hadn't looked in on the lieutenant for several days, and that last occasion hadn't been too pleasant. The patient had been feeling poorly. The invalid's presence on the outpost wasn't convenient.

The other men wounded in the wagon-train fracas were up and around again. But what was he to do with an amputee — especially one who was a general's son? A double-amputee, at that, and all because of a damn-fool stunt.

As soon as the shavetail was fit to travel, Marcus planned to send him back to Fort Sill in one of the deep-bottomed freight wagons. Hayes Bingham's army career was over. The young man could no longer ride or shoot, and had a hard time even pushing a pen. What disability would eventually mean to Hayes — or his father — wasn't Marcus's problem.

As soon as the Cantonment on the Sweetwater was solid and secure, there'd be patrols to mount. Leaping Wolf had to be hunted down. The hostiles' supply of firearms had to be cut off. Travelers and herds would need protection during panhandle crossings. Major Cavanaugh had his own problems without worrying about Bingham.

The major walked past two lowly privates digging a latrine with spades. Chest-deep in the hole they'd dug, hampered by leg irons, chains and twenty-pound iron balls, both were sweating like hogs. It was Orly and Kendall, still working out their punishment for fighting. Neither soldier looked in good humor. Marcus moved on and entered the hospital by the unpainted slab door.

"Well, Major Cavanaugh, and good day to you." The surgeon glanced up through iron-rimmed spectacles from his patient, a mule-kicked private fresh from stable detail. Pike's eyes twinkled. The owner of the cracked rib scowled sourly.

"Good morning, Major Pike. I hear your other patient in the back room is getting ants in his pants."

"You hear correctly," the surgeon replied. "Young Bingham's doing well from a physical point of view — infection staved off, nice clean stumps of both the arm and the leg. But the lad's feelings, that's another thing. Although I think by now I've managed to talk him out of suicide."

"He's still despondent?"

"Well, laying in that bed of pain is no picnic. He's still weak, even after all this time. Still hurting. Since I'm busy with kick abrasion here, Major, why don't you stroll on back and visit the lieutenant?"

"I'll just do that."

Marcus walked into the second room. The light was dimmer through drawn curtains, and smelled less of liniment and more of something less definable. It was not body waste, or seeping pus and blood on bandages in need of changing, but the stench of sickness. The man reclining on the rope cot wasn't sturdy yet.

With the loss of his right arm and left leg, he was bitter about his fate, and to the Indian warriors who'd given him his wounds. Whether or not Hayes Bingham had a quarrel with himself for being with the emigrants when the attack came, Marcus wasn't sure.

"Major?"

The form in the corner was in shadow, but Marcus Cavanaugh could see that he was frail and haunted. His cheeks were drawn and his eyes were sunken, though they smoldered with a fire. He was partially propped up, clad in a nightshirt. No quilt or sheet covered him. It was hot and stuffy in the room.

Marcus moved closer. "It's me, all right, Lieutenant. You're looking better, I see." The last visit he'd made, the patient had been flushed with fever.

"Don't exaggerate, Major. I must look like hell. That's how I feel. Would you believe it? My missing limbs hurt me! Really hurt, as much as the raw stumps, which the sawbones says are healing." A weak snort issued from his slack mouth. "Calling Pike a sawbones — me! That's a joke, Major Cavanaugh. You aren't laughing."

"No."

"What I want is to get out of this godforsaken hole. I feel useless, and I don't like that. And I don't like the fact that I ventured from the advance party of soldiers at this outpost. I got word a lady friend was with the emigrant train that was on its way, and I couldn't wait to see Clementine. I have to pay for that, but I don't have to do it here. I request to be put on an eastbound wagon as soon as possible. I'm fit to travel that way at least."

"If the surgeon agrees, I've no objection."

"As soon as I'm out of here, you and this place can go to hell!"

"You say what you feel, Lieutenant. I won't argue."

"You damn well better not."

Marcus peered grimly at the peevish wreck. He said nothing for a moment, then finally, "Well, I guess I'll be going."

"Don't forget about shipping me east. I'm ready anytime."

"I won't forget. Good day, Lieutenant."

"Good day for me? Ha!"

Marcus exited.

Outside, it was hot, too, but at least the air was fresh. Marcus breathed deeply. Out on the parade ground, some listless dismounted drill went on. He could faintly hear a sergeant shouting, "Yer left, yer right, yer left . . . *halt!*" On the tall staff, the Stars and Stripes spanked in the steady wind. Sabine Gilliam, far away in the paddock, was grooming his favorite dun.

Hayes Bingham was an embittered fool. To hell with him, Marcus decided. He walked, almost with relief, toward the headquarters where his desk was piled with paperwork.

Weevil Jones and Jeb Abercrombie were the army's lowest of the low, buck-ass private recruits, enlisted less than a month before. Both hailed from the backwoods of Arkansas and had never gone to school. But they were alike in other ways, too — young, gangling and homely. Jones was pimply faced and slow-moving. Abercrombie's features were unmarked, but he walked — even ate — with all the speed of a spavined armadillo.

Now, in the sweat-popping furnace heat of midday, the men moved upstream along the bank of the Sweetwater. They made their way with acute sluggishness, lugging double-bitted axes. Tick-filled grass brushed their legs, and willow saplings whipped their bare arms leaving reddish welts. Mosquitoes and flies hummed about the men's faces, stinging often.

The two soldiers were on firewood detail. Cooking required such excursions daily. Choppers cut enough trees, hiked back to the outpost to fetch the mules and wagon, then tossed the wood aboard. Once it was transported to the yard outside the kitchen, it was unloaded and the split faggots were stacked. It was hot, hard labor.

The Arkansawyers hadn't been on wood-chopping duty long, but it already felt long enough. Every day meant a farther hike to reach standing trees, especially since they had to compete with the crews who were gathering roof poles. Today they found themselves a half mile from the outpost, with just insects and snakes to keep them company.

"Up ahead there's a tree fit ta chop," Abercrombie muttered, pointing.

"So 'tis. May's well go at her."

The cottonwood stood fifty yards further along. Just beyond it, the prairie rolled slightly into a dip. A miniature gulch had been created by occasional rain run-off, and it harbored a clump of stunted mesquite. The buildings of the compound were clearly visible in the distance.

They left their rifles at their last stand of tree stumps. The long guns were heavy and unwieldy when a man carried an axe. The privates wore side-arms, however, in long flap-holsters. These were the Colt .45-caliber six-guns, the best weapons either had ever carried.

When they spotted the lone Indian, Jones and Abercrombie froze. The figure sat on his standing pony a dozen yards off, in the open and unconcealed. His garb wasn't particularly warlike. He wore an antelope-skin shirt, leggings and a headband with a feather. His black hair hung in braids down his chest. He appeared not to have glimpsed the soldiers nearby, being so intent on watching those in the distance. His gaze was fixed on the outpost and the activity there. His shiney new rifle rested across his mount's withers.

Abercrombie was about to say something, but

Jones's quick gesture cut him off. Moving his hand across his throat and pointing at the redskin, he communicated a foolhardy plan.

Abercrombie drew his heavy .45. Jones followed suit. They begin stalking the Indian. Jones ghosted along the scraggly screen of mesquite brush. He'd used the same technique hunting javalinas in the Ozarks, and moved without a sound. Abercrombie kept to lower ground along the stream, shielded by tree clumps. With each passing step, the troopers became further separated.

Birds, aware of the trespassers' presence, ceased warbling or silently took to the air. Crickets stopped chirping. The only sound was the occasional stamping of the Comanche's impatient pony. It was the unnatural quiet that alerted Swift Deer to his danger. The dark eyes, set above the coppery cheekbones, narrowed and began to scan. He caught the flash of a blue sleeve through a spray of dusty leaves and jerked his mount's head around with its jaw rope. As the pony wheeled, he brought up his gun. Weevil Jones found himself peering down the cavelike bore.

"Jesus Christ," he yelped, firing his pistol from his hip. He missed.

The Comanche's Winchester boomed, and the Colt leapt from the trooper's hand, smashed by the bullet. Jones spun away, clutching his wrenched forearm. Abercrombie's gun began to talk. From the cover of an ancient deadfall, the Arkansawyer fired swiftly, but by then, the spotted pony was charging straight for his dig-in.

"A-ah-iiee!" the redskin screamed.

Abercrombie rolled from the path of the pounding hooves just in time. He was hit in the side as the warrior tore by, firing the deadly Winchester.

Punched to the earth, the trooper flopped back, his head striking a log. Swift Deer jacked his rifle's action, ramming home another round. He'd veered the horse, and bore down again.

Jones ran up, thrusting a fallen limb he'd snatched from the ground at the Indian's pony. Like a lance, the brittle wood smashed into the animal's soft nose. The pony screamed and sunfished, but the warrior, horseman that he was, expertly managed to kept his seat. Hissing his rage, he turned his gun on the trooper threat nearest him. The hammer dropped and the rifle cracked. A bullet drove into Weevil Jones's head and exploded out the back. The red man gave an exultant cry.

The Comanche's triumph was cut short, however. Far down the stream, almost a thousand yards away, a deep-pitched boom roared out, followed by a gray puff of gunsmoke. A .45-caliber slug, propelled by seventy grains of black powder, grazed the redskin's scalp. Swift Deer threw his arms up and pitched from his pony to the grass.

The unmoving form sprawled beside the corpse of Jones, and several yards from Abercrombie. The trooper propped himself up, and counted himself lucky, though he was bleeding and the pain felt like a devil's prod. Shouts rang above the moan of the wind, and he could see uniformed figures on the run, the other troopers who'd been working along the Sweetwater.

"Wh-who?" Abercrombie grunted when the first troops ran up.

"Only one man could've made that shot. Devlin!"

The troopers were in a celebrating mood. "You had

to've seen Harley Devlin around the barracks, Ab. Wiry feller with dark skin and a long nose. Gets promoted to corporal reg'lar-like, but allus gets busted back agin? Sergeants hate him on account of his talkin' back?"

Abercrombie shook his head. Devlin came up lugging his hefty trapdoor-loader. He gripped its eight-pound weight as if juggling a feather. "Ayeh, feller, you're damn lucky I set my eye up this way. Was diggin' clay back there, but I had Betsy here to hand like always."

"That shooting?"

A kind of modesty tinged Harley Devlin's freckled face. "Think nothin' of it. I used to do it always 'bout like that in my days as a market hunter in the Montana camps. Shot plenty o' game in the mountains for the miners to eat. But Christ! Look there! The red varmint, he ain't dead."

He started to ram a fresh cartridge into the firing chamber, but a horse galloped up and a harsh voice barked an order. "If that Indian is still alive, don't kill him!"

The eyes of a dozen surprised troopers flew to Captain Phil Turnbo. "Huh?"

"What the hell?"

"Not splatter the damned red nigger's brains?"

Turnbo was gesturing for them to tie up the unconscious prisoner. "My feeling goes like this, men. The major himself may want to talk to this one." He pointed. "His rifle on the ground there! See? It's one of those factory-new Winchesters!"

Chapter Five

From the parade ground in front of headquarters, Marcus watched the wagon and its escort move off toward the east. Overhead, the Stars and Stripes flapped in the unceasing wind. A whirlwind swept dust into a funnel and danced in the receding column's wake. The shavetail puppy, Lieutenant Hayes Bingham, was headed back for Sill, and as far as Cavanaugh was concerned, it was good riddance to him.

Marcus rubbed sweat from his face, straightened his kepi across his forehead and glanced about. He spied the alert sentries on the outpost's perimeter. His order last evening, doubling their number, had been immediately carried out. After the incident involving the lone Comanche, greater-than-normal vigilance was demanded. A Company had lost two men — one dead, one wounded — though the wounded trooper would return to duty in a few short weeks.

From where he stood, Marcus could see the tool

shed where the troublesome warrior had been confined. In front, a guard with his rifle on his shoulder slowly paced. Pike had cleaned the Indian's head wound before the brave came to. It was the major's notion to let the prisoner stew a few days before questioning him on where his band got its rifles.

The troopers had been damn fools to try to take the warrior by themselves, as Private Abercrombie had learned. And the commander intended to keep his eye on the marksman named Devlin. His kind of skill was valuable, if the man's unruliness could be contained. Now that the repairs to the cantonment were nearly complete, Cavanaugh's new priority was a resumption of drills and a tightening of discipline to mold a fighting force.

Regular target practice for the troopers would be a good idea, too, even though the army frowned on the waste of cartridges. Ammunition — like foodstuffs — had to be conserved on the frontier, though the forts back east always seemed to have plenty. The country's military machine was full of political logrolling and graft, Marcus Cavanaugh well knew. But the army was his life, and duty was his personal god.

Since the day that he'd graduated from West Point, Marcus had worn the army uniform proudly. As he strode through swirling dust on a griddle-hot parade in remote Texas to a headquarters made of spongy sod blocks, he showed the same straight-backed snap as he did parading on the mall in Washington.

As he turned to mount the step, the major cast a last glance over his shoulder. Out across the flat land, a plume of dust rose against the dazzling sky, approaching at about the speed of a cantering horse. Marcus's attention focused on the movement, and he shielded his squinting eyes. The rider, by his blue blouse, yellow neckerchief and buff campaign hat, was a trooper. It was probably a member of a patrolling scout troop, sent back in as a messenger.

The sergeants would get the word from the runner and relay it to their commander. There was no real reason to linger in the sun when he could be attacking his backlogged paperwork. The major crossed the threshold in a stride, and within a minute, he was behind his desk. Whenever the goings-on outside interested him, he could look through the open window.

The rider galloped into the compound with a shout and a wave, and reined up in front of a hasty gathering of noncoms. Foremost of these was Patrick Keogh.

"And what news do ye be bringin' us, man?"

The sun-browned soldier, Private McMurchison, stepped from his saddle in front of the first Sergeant.

"You maybe won't believe this, Sergeant, but it's true, I swear! The lieutenant could hardly believe his eyes at first, but he sent me back to fetch the post word. Two freight wagons are on the move this way, and'll likely get here today. Here's where they're a-headin', right enough. And there's buildin' boards packed, and paulins to rig a makeshift roof, and women — "

"Whoa!"

"Huh?"

"Slow down, me lad," Keogh slurred in his rich County Kildare brogue. "Yer talkin' fast, and yer talkin' confused, like ye been out too long under the sun. I think I grasped the part ye said about the wagons on their way, but there was somethin' else?"

38

"Women," the horse soldier repeated. There were a number of scoffs vented. The private, however, stuck by his story. "Yeah, I said women, that's females, that's fancy gals, you can call the bevy what you will! There's a few drivers to work the mules, and it's claimed they'll stay in these parts a day or two throwin' up a house, leastwise that's what the boss of the outfit claims."

"Build a house? Near the post here?" Keogh asked. "This is what you rode back here to report?"

"In case the commanding officer needs to get ready or somethin'. I reckon me'n the other sojers are a-goin' to like havin' the fancy gals to enjoy. And a real dram shop for drinkin' whiskey and gamblin' and — "

"Care for your horse, Private. I'll be tellin' the major all this. He'll be wantin' to know, I'm sure. It'll mean some changes he's likely to be concerned about."

"Yes sir!" McMurchison saluted and led his lathered and thirsty animal away.

Keogh shrugged to Corporals Foxx and Malthus, then turned on his heel and marched to headquarters as fast as his bowed cavalryman's legs could take him. He burst through the orderly room and into Marcus's office.

"Yes, Sergeant?"

"It's come like it was bound to all along, Major! 'Tis said it'll be arrivin' yet today! A saloon for alongside the post! Gamblin' tables! Whores!"

"The inevitable hog ranch?"

"Yes, sir!" the sergeant replied with a grin that stretched from ear to ear.

Marcus nodded placidly. "Well, when the proprietor turns up, Sergeant, make him aware of the Indian danger, if you please. Although he already realizes the risks of the business he's in, I'm sure."

"I suppose so, sir!"

"Inform Lieutenant Ambrose that I'll be expecting him to inspect the new place."

"I will, sir!"

"A complication to life here at the cantonment, Sergeant, albeit a minor one."

Lieutenant Nate Ambrose, slat thin, ramrod straight and with his uniform tunic freshly sponged, watched the workmen put the last touches on the crudely built saloon. This amounted to stout oak shutters that had been brought on the wagons. Too thick to be penetrated by bullets and arrows, they'd be easily swung shut at the first sign of attack.

Quite a few loopholes had been cut in the boards to let folks shoot out, and the roof as well as sides of the low structure was matted with fireproof sod. The place squatted on the flats, well away from trees and gullies that might shield attackers. It was fortified as well as it could be — of that, Ambrose was satisfied.

While the hammering and fitting went on, it occurred to Ambrose to view the whole shebang once from the other side. He didn't care to involve himself at the moment with the knot of females he saw clustered in a wagon's shade. Those four had to be the fancy ladies mentioned by Keogh, a tired-looking lot in bright dresses, their faces tinged with rouge. He was surprised to see most of them were somewhat homely. Then he remembered what happened to pretty gals out on the frontier. They soon became wives.

Not choosing to exert himself under the high sun, the young officer made his way with measured steps in the opposite direction, past the second of the conveyances that had brought the party. Just as Ambrose stepped around the tailgate, he heard raised voices, a man's and a woman's, but it was too late to stop.

The man he'd seen before, going about the building site. The woman was unfamiliar. And from the two flushed faces they wore, they'd been arguing hard. At the sight of the young officer, though, frowns turned to artificial smiles. The fellow in the frock coat and string tie spoke up cordially.

"Why, Lieutenant. Welcome to my premises and hello."

The coat was a neutral dust color, as was the man's hat. He was clean shaven, except for a flowing black mustache above a knife-slit mouth. At the moment, the man was smiling. "My name's Kyle, Lieutenant, Jack Kyle, lately of the fair town of Fort Smith. And this lady is my associate, Miss Retta Cantrell." He fished a cheroot from the pocket of a gray vest and peered at Ambrose expectantly.

Ambrose obliged by introducing himself. "Lieutenant Nate Ambrose. Hail from Arkansas, do you, Mr. Kyle? I believe our major served there for a time."

"Actually, Jack doesn't hail from there, Lieutenant," the woman put in. "What he meant to say was, he's most recently run an establishment there. Much the same as the one he aims to open down the trail from your fort."

"Actually, it isn't a fort, Miss Cantrell, but rather an outpost. A fort is base to a full regiment, that's twelve companies — as much as a thousand men if the regiment is fully manned."

"Oh. I didn't know."

Ambrose studied Retta Cantrell carefully for the first time. A tumble of fiery red hair haloed a pretty face, the most prominent feature of which was a pair of flashing green eyes. There were fine lines at the sides of her mouth. She was perhaps a few years older than the officer. As to stature, she was tall, and she wore a plain dress with a high and modest neckline.

He became aware that he was staring when Kyle spoke again. "If you were sent here by your post commander, Lieutenant, you can report that I intend to offer decent whiskey and beer at a fair price, considering the risks. Call my place a hog ranch if you want, but the females offered ain't hogs at all. They're the youngest and healthiest as could be found who were willin' to work way out here. Ain't that right, Retta?"

The woman sniffed. "I have nothing to do with that end of the business, Kyle. Letting on that I do doesn't make it so."

He still fingered the crooked, unlit stogy. Now he jammed it into his mouth. "I'll try and remember how you feel, Miss High-and-Mighty."

"Do that."

Nathan Ambrose cleared his throat. "What I really intend to report to my superior officer, folks, is that you've put up a fairly defensible structure in your saloon. That's good, considering the Comanche threat here. There was a hostile redskin shot yesterday just a few yards from this spot. But be careful — that is, watchful — and you should be all right. I guess I don't need to wish you good luck. With all the hard-drinking soldiers hereabouts, you're bound to have enough."

42

Retta Cantrell turned to Ambrose. "Don't be a stranger to the place yourself, Lieutenant. I'll be running the gambling layout in the back, and you can count on fair, square treatment."

"I'm not much of a gambler, Miss Cantrell, but I'll remember." He glanced up at the setting sun. "Well, I'd best be getting back. I'll say good day to you both." He touched his kepi's visor in politeness to the woman, then turned on his heel and strode off.

When he was out of sight behind the wagon, he heard the talk between the two take up again. He couldn't make out the words, but the tone was harsh. Kyle and Retta Cantrell obviously didn't get along. It was none of his business, really, but interesting to know.

Across the barren Llano Estacado, the furnace wind moaned just as it always did. The plain baked across the entire horizon under the sky's glare. Even the wildlife hid to endure the daytime heat. It was an arid ocean of brittle grass, unbroken but for a broad, depressed bowl, where the ground sloped gently for well over a half mile. In the middle of the dip was a dark area of mud surrounding a pond. The last rain had fallen months ago.

Down the slope and toward the welcome water, two horsemen trotted. They had to fight their mounts and, their throats parched and swollen, their own eagerness as well. Both men wore dust-caked Stetsons, denim pants and faded checked shirts. The saddles were cattle-working rigs, and the animals were cow ponies. Bedrolls were tied behind their cantles, and large round canteens swung in front of their thighs. The canteens had been emptied yesterday. The men were allowing the horses' noses to lead them to water. They were very lucky that they had found it nearby.

Cowboys returning south from a cattle drive to Dodge often met hardship, but these two men had found more than their share. They'd lost one pack horse in a flash flood on the Canadian River, and broke its leg in a gopher hole. They'd become short of grub on the trail, and spent ammunition on elusive game. Bob Everett's Remington six-gun had lost a firing pin. Cuff Ward's current mount, Shaky, had come up lame and had to travel slowly.

And meanwhile, the herd owner and the outfit's ramrod rode home comfortably on the train. That route was east via the Katy line to Kansas City, then south to San Antonio. Some of the drivers who'd done well gambling at Dodge could afford the quick way, too, but Cuff had lost most of his trail pay playing faro. Bob had dropped his wad at dice. Now they made their way south on horseback through the heart of Comanche country. Although they hadn't seen an Indian yet, they worried plenty. And they still had a long way to go.

"Buffalo wallow, you claim?" Cuff Ward asked. He was a cowboy of the black race, too young to recall the great bison herds.

"Yeah, that's what this is." Bob Everett was older, with a salt-and-pepper thatch under his hat and a salt-and-pepper beard. Just turned forty, he'd spent the years since he was sixteen on Texas ranches. He was what they called an old hand. He wished he had more to show for his experience than calloused hands and rump.

"Hot damn!" Cuff whooped. "Water, and it ain't even rained."

"Rain collects in these 'cause they're low-lyin'," Bob explained. "Now and again you find one so big it's a lake all year-round. They do beat creeks that'll dry up most summers."

Cuff drew a sleeve across his sweaty brown brow. The frayed fabric sopped moisture up like a sponge. Both horses required firm reining as the scent of water tickled their nostrils.

"I ain't able to picture so many buffalo as'd be able to tramp down this."

Bob Everett spat dust. "Shit, man, it weren't done at once, but over the years. Lots of years. The critters sought mud after rains so's to coat the hair on 'em, keep the flies off. The herds was big, though. Millions of buffalo. Now mostly killed off. Makes the redskins mad as hell."

The wiry quarter horses were at the wallow water's bank. The cowboys drew up. "You reckon there's any Injuns close by now, Bob?"

"They need to drink, same as us. We'll need to keep our eyes peeled." And so saying, he cast his gaze about, glimpsing movement on the tramped wallow's high lip! "Cuff, I think I seen — Christ! Grab your shootin' iron!"

A ferocious cry rent the air, and a row of warriors rode their ponies into view. It was an impressive sight but terrifying. Feathers on headdresses and brandished lances, bows and firearms bobbed. On signal, rounds burst from the muzzles of rifles all down the long row, and slugs chewed ground near the cowboys.

"Ride like hell!" Bob Everett hollered.

"Our horses is tired! Ain't had no drinks!"

"Ride like hell!"

The twenty-some warriors who followed Leaping Wolf tore downslope and splashed through mud. Water splashed from the hooves of the savage riders' mounts. Bullets sprayed the air about the cowboys' ears.

"Christ, Bob! Christ!" Bob Everett's horse crashed to earth, shot.

Cuff Ward jerked his reins, and Shaky's head came around. The young black cowboy gave spur. He charged the redskin hoard venting yells of challenge. Both men opened up with their own Winchesters, prepared for their last stand.

Chapter Six

The situation was desperate and grew worse with each passing minute. Cuff Ward and Bob Everett were forced to battle with more than a score of men. Flight was impossible, with Bob's horse shot. Still, the black cowboy named Cuff thought he'd make a try.

Giving spur to his rangy chestnut, he rode down on his partner's position, halfway up the sloping side of the buffalo wallow, a hundred yards from the muddy center. Already the charging warriors had passed that point. Amid a constant zinging of bullets, Cuff dipped low in the saddle, leaned down the mount's off side and extended an arm. Bob Everett stood in a crouch, prepared to leap up as the horse swept past.

"Grab me, pard," he shouted.

Cuff gritted his teeth and nodded curtly. The chestnut thundered near and Bob jumped, snagging the surging pommel in his grip. At the same instant, Ward's strong hand wrapped around his shirt and lifted him. The cowboy clung to the running animal's sleek side, his face pressed to its saddle and his fingers locked around the horn. Cuff Ward clutched Everett's belt tightly. Without flagging, the horse tore back up the slope on fleet hooves.

Behind the cowboys, the Indian's cries of anger rang out. Firing redoubled, and the Comanches' ponies spread out to either side, galloping to cut off their quarry. In the blizzard of arrows and bullets, Cuff Ward's shoulder was struck. The same volley brought down the big chestnut. The animal gouted blood from a bullet deep in its lung. It fell in a heap, kicking in spasms. Thrown clear, the two men stumbled and dropped flat.

As the tide of hostiles bore down and surrounded them, the cowboys worked their Winchesters until the barrels grew hot. Well-aimed shots punched the two braves from their ponies — this while Cuff had only one good arm, and with Bob Everett nursing a game leg.

The white man and the black man lay between the dead horse and the thrashing chestnut, which provided some shielding, but not too much. Suddenly, the hurt animal shrieked and collapsed. With its death came a violent venting of the beast's bowels that filled the air with a stench. The cowboys fought on without letup, drawing beads on the galloping warriors who circled close and dealing death.

Indian corpses littered the ground, but the surviving redskins whooped and kept up their fire. An arrow pierced Bob Everett's forearm, and he dropped his rifle. Another bullet found Cuff's bulky form, this time through the lower chest. He slumped momentarily, then roused himself, jacked the rifle's action once more, fired left-handed and missed.

The leader of the party, Leaping Wolf, was tall for a Comanche at nearly six feet. With arms thicker than most men's necks, he wielded prodigious strength. The eagle feathers that he wore made a brave show as he bore down on the besieged pair. He rode his pony with lack of caution, for he knew his medicine was good this day. Believing that his bare copper skin was immune to bullets, he wielded his long gun with skill.

Everett viewed the big Indian bearing down over his Colt's bright sights. He squeezed the trigger, his muzzle pointed at the Indian's broad, thick chest. At a range of ten feet, his expert aim couldn't fail. The Colt misfired.

"Goddamn!" Bob Everett swore. Then he was struck by the enormous running pony, and flew backward, his arms windmilling. He landed sprawled on the slope, unprotected, the wind knocked from his frame. He looked up. Indians ringed him, their weapons pointing. Everett resolved to die, but he wasn't that lucky.

Warriors leaped from their mounts and ran to him, kicking his six-gun from his hand and pinning him with powerful hands. Nearby he could hear the frantic grunts of his pard, Cuff Ward. The black man was receiving rough treatment, too. The two cowboys were dragged into the open, away from the dead horses, and the real pummeling commenced. Fists, moccasined feet, and the Indians' rawhide quirts fell into play. The captives were beaten for what seemed a painful eternity. Their troubles hadn't even started.

Leaping Wolf stalked nearby. The war leader shouted orders in a gutteral tone. Several followers seized Cuff Ward's limbs. They stretched them wide, while two more Comanches slashed off his remaining clothes. Within a minute, the tough black man was stripped, his wrists and ankles pegged securely to the ground. Low moans escaped Cuff's lips. He bucked and tugged at his bonds.

Everett, too, was swiftly bound, but his arms were tied behind his back with rawhide thongs. Instead of being pushed flat, he was forced to sit upright and watch. Dried dung was thrust between Cuff's legs, flint and steel produced, and a tiny fire kindled. The flames were small and smokeless, but strategically placed. Cuff's private parts singed slowly at first, then more rapidly. Soon his body hair ignited. He broke silence with a piercing roar of agony.

The Comanches laughed, and a few notched steel-tipped arrows to their bowstrings. One haughty savage drew his bow to its extremity. He poised a moment, shoulder muscles corded, then released the bowstring. It twanged. The elm-wood bow was strengthened with antelope horn. It drove its arrow deep into Ward's naked thigh. The tortured man's screams redoubled.

Bob Everett witnessed the start of the torture session.

The unsprung freight wagon jolted on a prairie hummock, and Hayes Bingham felt a twinge of pain. He cursed. On the seat beyond the canvas bonnet, the driver cursed, too, and plied his whip. The mule team jerked the wagon forward, and yet more pain was inflicted on the amputee. This time Hayes Bingham gritted his teeth in silence. Since he was alone, he saw no use in fussing.

The trip was a boring and miserable hell. He'd had a notion before leaving the Cantonment on the Sweetwater that it would be a relief to be moving, but it hadn't turned out that way. The jouncing wagon wasn't doing well without a road, and miles of prairie weren't unfolding fast enough. The stumps of his lost arm and leg ached constantly.

It did the lieutenant no good to know his maiming came from being at the wrong place at the wrong time, willfully in disobedience of orders. He'd had no business courting Clementine Drury. His duty at the time had lain with his troops and the outpost.

He wrenched his body about, knocking his stump against his knee. Hurt shot up his shoulder like a splash of hot acid. Still, it didn't hurt as much as it had just days before. He was forced to admit that with less and less physical discomfort, guilt set in. What would become of him, with his military career cut short? Endure family pity for unending years? Wear a hook for a hand and hickory peg leg?

"Damn!"

Surgeon Pike had given him painkiller for the journey to Fort Sill. Bingham groped beside the cot with his one and only hand. He came up with the small, brown glass bottle with the jammed-down cork. Laudanum. At the moment the physical pain wasn't bad, but the mental anguish was. Clasping the bottle tight in his left fingers, he bit the cork and tugged it free. Letting it roll among the bedclothes, Bingham thrust the bottle to his seeking lips. He swallowed the liquid.

It was more than enough. Pike had warned him of the addictive nature of the opiate, but Hayes Bingham needed to be soothed badly. His pain was too much to bear, and he didn't care if he'd be forced to pay later. Sweet drowsiness closed in, lulled him. His chin dropped to his chest.

The driver peeked back through the bonnet. Then he turned to his team and shook his head. "He might be an officer, but he ain't no man," the private muttered. "A man can stand a bit o' bad luck and pain."

Cuff Ward screamed his last in midafternoon. During hours of torment, his taut body was shot full of arrows that had been aimed at non-vital parts. He'd been kept alive in order to suffer to the utmost, and he'd done so. At last, he died from loss of blood from the wound that took his manhood.

Then the Comanche torturers turned to Bob Everett. The graying cowboy, stripped naked, was thrown down, and a rain of blows descended. He shrieked. Bones in his arms and legs were broken, war hatchets and stones doing work that produced hideous pain. The Indians mashed tender fingers and toes as well, and then began upon his unprotected face.

The victim was blinded with the sharp points of knives, and then his belly was slashed. The ingenious warrior Bear Tooth yanked out handfuls of intestines and started on them with his stone-headed hatchet. Soon the innards were mashed to mincemeat. And the screams of pure agony went on and on. As the sun dropped and the day lost brightness, Bob Everett gave up the ghost.

Leaping Wolf's cruel eyes watched, pleased, as the victims of his band's torture were scalped. The warriors claiming the grisly trophies shook them aloft. Blood sprayed from the scraps of crudely cut skin.

Gutteral grunts turned to whoops of triumph as the Indians sprang to their ponies' backs. They grasped the animals' jaw ropes and urged them north, toward the waiting lodges of blue-coat soldiers at the Cantonment on the Sweetwater.

Chapter Seven

Marcus Cavanaugh walked faster than normal when he left his quarters. At the other end of the compound, the companies' trumpeter signaled the morning mounting of the guard. The major had stopped back at the small house after breakfast mess, issued orders to his striker regarding cleaning chores, and prepared for the morning's first important task. He didn't expect it to be a particularly pleasant one.

At the corner of the commissary building, he met Keogh and Turnbo. The two officers and the noncom swung along the path toward where the Indian prisoner was being held.

The slight misting of dew had burned off in the early sunshine. The day was shaping up as usual, exceedingly warm. The trio expected the tight shed to have accumulated strong odors from the Comanche. Sabine Gilliam had filled them in on some of the customs of the tribe. According to the breed scout, typical Comanches never bathed from birth until their dying day.

"We'll have the man brought into the yard for the interrogation, Captain," Marcus said. "Sergeant, make sure there are plenty of troopers standing by with guns. Part of the plan is to intimidate this Indian to help loosen his tongue."

Keogh snorted. "Sure, if by that ye mean put fear in him, remember something, Major. The savage don't abide by no Lord, 'cept maybe lightning and sacred animals and such. And his kind are trained not to let on to pain or fear." The bulky noncom shook his head dubiously. "So says Gilliam, if ye don't believe me. I'm thinking the redskin just might choose not to talk with us at all."

Marcus spoke to Turnbo as well as the sergeant. "This is something we have to do. You were right to save his life, Captain. The source of the raiders' new guns, it's got to be revealed. If you can think of a better way?"

"Of course I can't, Major Cavanaugh. We have to work with what we've got." He looked ahead. "Ah, Gilliam is at the shed ahead of us."

No fewer than eight troopers clutching Springfields also stood by alertly. They wore bleak frowns under tilted kepis and came to attention as the officers walked up.

"Mornin', Major," Gilliam said, saluting like the others. "Ready to get started?"

"I believe we're all ready as we'll ever be. Unbolt the door. Fetch our red friend out."

It was done. A minute later the copper-skinned brave, his wrists bound, blinked in the glare. His chunky torso bulged in his buckskins and he stood on short, bowed legs. He looked unsteady, however, and his eyes were clouded. Marcus glared at him, and he glared back.

Marcus knew the notorious reputation of the Comanche, as did all the white men behind him. Said to be the most skilled horsemen on earth, they were reputed to be able to shoot an arrow in a buffalo's dense flesh with an elm bow while galloping full tilt. But the Indian in front of them wasn't in robust health. The furrowed bullet graze across his brow was scabbed, but still ran with pus. He'd torn the bandage away and got dirt into the sore. Nor had he thrived on blue-coats' food.

In spite of it, the warrior managed an arrogant stance and stare. "Want him beat on with rifle stocks, Major?" Sabine Gilliam queried. "Could soften him a bit, maybe, but there's no guarantees."

"Let's simply begin the questioning. Can you find out his name?"

The scout shrugged. Then the rattle of the Comanche language sounded in his throat, the liquid intonation so different from the Shoshonean-based Cheyenne tongue that Marcus had once tried learning. Apparently the Indian was willing that his captors know his identity.

"Says his people call him Hona-ka. Swift Deer," Gilliam interpreted. "Claims to be a brave man among raiders led by Leaping Wolf."

"Where is Leaping Wolf right now?"

The scout and the Indian spoke for a minute.

"He says somewhere to the west or south of here. The sundown land. What the old Spaniards called Llano Estacado. Powerful lot of territory out there, Major. Army patrols go out huntin', they'll come up a mile short and a dozen shy most times. And if they do

56

strike pay dirt and sniff Comanche, they'd end up ambushed."

"We need more than Swift Deer is telling."

"You bet."

"The other thing that interests me, Gilliam, is those rifles. Where the emigrant wagons were attacked, you found repeaters, new Winchesters held by Indian dead. When Swift Deer was caught scouting the cantonment, he carried the same kind of gun. Ask him where Leaping Wolf is buying those firearms."

This time the scout used sign lingo as well as talk. But when he paused to listen, there was no response. The Comanche turned morose.

"Appears he's took it on himself not to talk no more."

"We need his information," Marcus said flatly.

Captain Phil Turnbo, by no means of puny build, stepped close. "With your permission, Major." The officer's sorrel mustache twitched as his arm shot out and pushed the red man against the shed. "Damn you, redskin! Settlers — fine men and women — are dead on account of some renegade trader's greed! The government aims to run the man down, peg his hide to the wall! And you're going to help us find him, Indian!" Turnbo caught a handful of Swift Deer's lousy hair, then jerked his head around. He cocked his free fist and readied a blow to the face.

"Hold on!" Marcus snapped. "I mean it, Captain!"

Phil Turnbo froze.

The Comanche glared at his captors with defiant hate.

"He's a murdering savage, Major," Turnbo hissed. "Likely took part in that settler massacre! Might be the very one who shot Hayes Bingham! And if yet more of those new rifles get in redskin hands, there'll be more — "

"Let go of the Indian for now, Turnbo." Marcus Cavanaugh's blue eyes were ice. All around him troopers, weapons ready, gaped. "It's an order. Don't forget yourself, Captain."

The captain, his rugged jaw working, loosened his grip. Swift Deer reeled a bit, then stood. Keogh and Gilliam hemmed him in beside the shed's door.

"We'll continue the questioning in another session," Marcus stated. "Tomorrow. Same time. Same shed. I have no doubt that Swift Deer will break." He turned to Turnbo. "Report to me at headquarters before next meal call, Captain. I'll make our chat brief."

"Yes, sir."

Swift Deer had been shoved back into his cell, with the massive bar dropped across the door.

"Soldiers, you're dismissed. Except for the one man who'll stand guard here." Marcus returned the troopers' salutes, as did the noncom and the captain. The yard quickly emptied after that. Marcus, straight-backed and grim, stalked off alone.

"You reckon he's really got somethin' up his sleeve?" Gilliam asked Keogh. The sergeant shrugged.

"I dunno, scout, but the old man, he don't like beatings done. 'Twas the same with him at Fort Bowie and Fort Supply, I've heard tell."

"Hell of a way for an officer to act. Most of 'em do discipline with hickory spoke and whip. Even sometimes order the branding iron used."

"That ain't the style of Marcus Cavanaugh, me man."

58

Under its low, pole-beamed roof, the barroom reeked of cheap whiskey and spilled beer, cheap tobacco smoke, the perfume of whores and the sweat of fifty half-drunk men. These were the troopers of C and D Companies. Lieutenant Lorne Hazelcrest's F Company was in the field on patrol. They made a rowdy roomful and raised a chaotic din. The foul air irritated people's throats like poison jimson weed. There was music from discordant banjo and jew's-harp. Every once in a while a game wheel spun and clattered. There were two bars in the saloon — one enlisted men's, one officers' — but they were duplicates. In a country short of wood, buffalo hides, dried-stiff, were laid across upright empty barrels.

The lowly bar was thronged, but the elite one was far from it. Only four officers and eight noncoms currently served at the outpost. Phil Turnbo nursed a brandy bottle that, over the hours, he'd very nearly emptied. Nate Ambrose, who'd shaved his face since supper, made small talk with the dour surgeon, Pike.

"This place is built like a redoubt," Ambrose said. "Look at the sandbags placed along the walls. And those loopholes for firing through. Hell, the roofs even have crude embrasures. Did you see 'em up there?"

The medical man tossed down Old Overholt — a double measure of the potent Irish rye. "Well, it's Indian country out here, isn't it?" He'd drunk five glasses of liquor, but his voice wasn't even slurred. "The feeling of safety's a good one, I'd say. Damned comfortable."

Ambrose shook his head and sipped flat beer. He

studied Turnbo out of the corner of his eye. His fellow officer had an amazing capacity for liquor, he'd discovered back at Fort Sill. Still, he was one of the finest leaders that the younger man had known in his days in the army.

"How you doing over there, Phil?"

"Doing fine. Finishing up. 'Bout time for call to quarters to be blown over at the post. Can't ignore call to quarters, the soldiers' lullaby to send 'em to their bunks."

"Good thing, really, if we don't ignore it. Reveille being at five-thirty."

Across the room, a trooper who was sober thrust his head in through the door. "Figure to clear this place pronto, you army men! Was you outside here, you'd hear the trumpeter doin' his evenin' chore!"

There was grumbling, and there was tossing down of final drinks, but the tough troopers who wished to avoid being disciplined on the morrow got a move on. The hog ranch emptied rapidly. The frock-coated Jack Kyle, aided by his bartender, began the routine of extinguishing the coal-oil lamps.

"Abandoning that bottle?" Pike asked Turnbo.

"May as well. I'm not crazy about the stuff. Drink from boredom."

"I know well what you mean, my lad," the medical man agreed. "I've spent a lifetime in the army on the frontier, and I know what you mean."

The three officers separated outside the soddy's walls, with Turnbo and Pike ambling leisurely in the direction of the outpost. Their silhouettes were black against the moon-silvered ground. Ambrose lingered to gaze at the spectacular sweep of stars, but he heard the voices receding.

"Cavanaugh didn't come down hard on you, then?" the surgeon inquired.

"No. Just said Swift Deer was a savage, but *we* needn't be. That made sense when I thought about it."

The surgeon ambled off into the night.

"Isn't it Lieutenant Ambrose?"

Ambrose turned to see a woman's form. She approached, and they shared the shadows near the ink-black wall. "Miss Cantrell."

"That's me. Pretty sky, isn't it? I don't get to see a pretty sky enough. Just the smoky lamps inside most of the evening."

"And the tabletop where you deal cards. I was watching you in there."

She tossed her long red hair. "What do self-pitying folks say? 'Hard work, but it's a living'? "

They laughed together.

"Something like that."

They were completely alone now, with the troopers gone. Kyle and the barkeep Casey weren't about, and the glitter-gal quartet hadn't ventured outside.

"Miss Cantrell," Lieutenant Ambrose began.

"Call me Retta. And I'll call you Nathan, or Nate. You know, I liked you from the first, Nate. I wish that Kyle, that bastard, hadn't been present when we met. Then we might not have wasted so much time before we got really together."

"Er, Retta . . . I — "

"I'm going to invite you to the lean-to room I sleep in, back of the soddy, Nate. But I don't want you to misunderstand. I'm not at all one of the hogs at this hog ranch. I'm not generally available to men. Not at any price. I came out to this place to run the gambling end for Kyle. It's a way to make my San Francisco stake. Going there's my dream. I have nothing to do with the rest of Kyle's business. Not the soiled doves, nor the . . . other."

Ambrose wondered idly what the other might be, but then the sweet female scent of Retta Cantrell surged through his senses. He clasped her hand in his.

"It isn't far to my little room," the woman breathed. "Come on."

And he discovered that, indeed, it wasn't far at all.

Chapter Eight

The days in north Texas grew hotter and more miserable as the summer dragged along. When there was a storm, it blew up suddenly, with sheets of lightning striking through a leaden sky to drum-roll thunder. Torrential rain or fist-sized hail would come next, sometimes a howling tornado as well. But most of the time it was dry, gusty and hot. The Cantonment on the Sweetwater baked, the sod-building bricks turning into dust.

With the repairs complete, the men dragged through days of grinding routine. Mounted drill was followed by fatigue chores, followed by dismounted drill. And when the day wound down, there was off-duty stupor and drunkenness. The paymaster's wagon was late, and when it did arrive — to cheers — it carried the usual greenbacks. A private's thirteen-dollar-a-month wage lost a quarter of its printed value. This was so at the sutler's store for green soap and tobacco, and at the hog ranch for its liquor or its whores.

The main breaks from the monotony were the patrols, which were another kind of hell. Each meant a week or more of days on horseback, rocking in merciless butt-busting McClellans twenty-five miles per day. *Upton's Tactics* prescribed allowable distance, plus requirements for the cavalrymen's cantle pack of gear. From canteens to sets of hobbles, spare cartridges to hardtack rations, the manual dictated them all. And what the book said was done in any garrison under the command of Marcus Cavanaugh. The major was known as a stickler as much as for his stout sense of duty.

Tough but fair, Cavanaugh was the son of a long-dead judge who had grown up inspired by his father's ideals. Now he drove his men hard, but no harder than he drove himself, hence the regard held by him by his present officers, Lorne Hazelcrest, Nathan Ambrose and Philip Turnbo.

Lieutenant Hazelcrest rode at the head of the column of F Company. He was a dark, dour-faced man who, like many officers after the War Between the States, had been far too long in his present rank. But he hadn't let the army's policy of slow promotion embitter him much. If he was in an irritable mood, it was due to the chafing collar of his tunic. He'd developed a bothersome rash from the scratchy fabric, but he knew the men under him wore flannel clothing, too. No one had any choice but to endure.

Rooster tails of dust from the weary horses' hooves combined to create a cloud. Guidons listlessly twitched on their poles. The brutal sun smote the country.

Sol "Long Jaw" Phelps, the aged white scout, scratched his thatch of chin whiskers. "Look over there in the sky, Lieutenant. Can you see 'em?"

Black motes like flecks of ash floated far off above the plain. Lorne Hazelcrest squinted as he gauged the distance. "Four or five miles away, I'd say."

"That's about it." The graybeard shifted his tobacco quid and screwed up his abundantly wrinkled features. "Them buzzards has found somethin', all right. Mebbe dead coyote or antelope to eat. Else, it's Injun mischief."

"We'll ride that way," the officer said, signaling to the company with a waved gauntlet.

"I figured you'd be sayin' that, Lieutenant."

The column of dusty blue-coats pointed their mounts southwest. "Sergeant Neal!"

The noncom loped his mount into position beside the officer's. "Yes, sir?"

"Send flankers off to left and right. We may run into trouble over there. And, Phelps, take a ride out ahead, if you please. I want no chances taken today."

"Yes, *sir!*"

Neal cantered back along the file, calling out names of troopers. These men dropped out and, on direction, veered their mounts away from the main body. Like twin lines of ants on the great surface of the flat, the cavalry company moved. Against the quietness of the plain, only the squeak of saddles and the jingle of bit chains sounded.

They came upon the corpses at last, and the lieutenant called a stop. The big, ugly buzzards tearing at entrails glared balefully, then, gorged, launched into awkward, flopping flight. From the ranks behind him, Hazelcrest heard troopers retching. He had to agree that this, for grisliness, topped viewing the slain emigrants.

There'd been more of those unfortunate men, women and children, true. But these men had been killed by mutilation, slowly, so as to prolong awful pain. Hazelcrest could have used a strong drink of whiskey. But he was a long way now from the hog ranch and the remedy it dispensed.

Long Jaw Phelps gigged his roan into the tight circle that the troopers formed, rejoining the officer. His seamed face was lit up with excitement. "Them two dead 'uns that ya see all tore, they got done in by Comanches," he announced. "The kind of lightning-line decorations on the arrows shows that clear. And there's the style of slashin' so's to cripple victims in the afterlife. See, the hands, they ain't carved on, like the Kiowa'd be like to do."

"Comanches. Yes." Hazelcrest's attention had drifted to the far horizon, where some cottony clouds hung poised.

"As for the private parts sliced off and stuffed in the boys' mouths — "

"Wait a minute, won't you, Phelps?" Hazelcrest's hand flew to his field glasses, which he jammed to his eyes. "Well, I'll be damned! There's a warrior out on that plain, Phelps! You, too, Sergeant Neal, look over there! On a buckskin war pony, and I judge the range close to a thousand yards! Ain't that sharpshooter Devlin in the ranks? Fetch him here! On the double!"

It took less than a minute for the trooper to trot up. "Yes, sir?" It was the same wily, freckled face and he carried the same long rifle. Because he was riding, it was slung by a shoulder strap. The army didn't issue saddle scabbards, and likely never would.

"Devlin." Lorne Hazelcrest smiled wickedly. "I've been told what you can do with a gun, game-hunting

66

fashion. I want you to show me now."

"I see the Injun, Lieutenant. Won't try to shoot 'im from horseback, though. Too far. No use. I'll just lay me on the ground, and use a saddle to prop up Betsy's barrel." He dismounted stiffly. "Now, to test the air . . ." Devlin licked his finger, and held the digit up. The breeze cooled it on the windward side.

"The savage's, fixin' to ride off. Got to act fast!"

"If he joins Leaping Wolf's band, he'll tell them we're on their trail. Lay us open to surprise attack!"

Devlin stretched on the ground. Holding his breath, he drew a careful bead. A hush fell on the troopers standing about. Devlin's powerful rifle boomed.

Nearly a full quarter mile to the west, the warrior chest was ripped by lead. The spinning slug churned bone, muscle and lung tissue, and exploded the Comanche's heart. The Indian contorted with the impact, slumped and dropped from his pony. All around, grass rustled in the wind. The pony, spooked, trotted away swiftly.

"Nice work, Devlin," Lorne Hazelcrest said.

Phelps shook the marksman's hand vigorously. Devlin wore a grin.

"Mebbe you'll buy me a drink sometime, Mr. Phelps," he suggested easily.

"Mebbe so."

"Sergeant Neal," Lieutenant Hazelcrest snapped. "As soon as these torture victims can be buried, we'll get on the raiding Indians' trail. Let the troopers make the most of the time till we move out, smoking their pipes, relieving themselves."

"Yes, sir!"

"I aim to run those red devils into the ground if I

possibly can this trip, mister! And when we engage 'em, I want F Company to do themselves proud!"

Within a short half hour, the column was in the saddle again, following the sun west. In the same direction ran the distinct prints of the renegade Comanches' mounts.

Chapter Nine

Seated behind his desk at headquarters, Marcus Cavanaugh frowned. "So the Indians' trail petered out and you had to turn back?"

"There was stony ground for miles along the route they took, Major."

Lorne Hazelcrest was downcast. "Damn the savages and their wily ways! I'd have given an arm to've surrounded Leaping Wolf and wiped his band from the earth's face!" More quietly, he added, "Sir, excuse me for letting anger show."

"Ask Hayes Bingham about the sacrifice of a limb, Lieutenant. As for disappointment, it's natural under the circumstances. These things happen."

Through the window looking out on the parade, Marcus watched the declining sun. Soon the supper hour would arrive and the cantonment's bustle would wind down for the day. This had been another long one. From the first moment F Company rode in, the men's fatigue had shown in thirty haggard faces.

The dismount had lacked snap. Plenty of grumbling rolled through the stable yard.

The most sour look of all had belonged to Lorne Hazelcrest. And yet the officer had put on a better face than he felt, and hurried over to report. He'd put the facts to his commander bluntly, and they spelled one thing — failure. He'd failed to kill Leaping Wolf or bring the Comanche leader in.

The facts showed again that the war leader was formidable. He knew how to strike, and how to vanish into hiding. He was an accomplished guerrilla tactician. He was the greatest menace that settlers and travelers in the region could face.

"The men who'd been riding south who were killed," Marcus clarified. "Cattle drivers returning from the railhead, you say?"

"That's pretty certain from their saddles and accoutrements, Major."

"And that lone warrior who was picked off. He carried a brand-new rifle?"

"Winchester repeater. Yes, sir."

"Damn, but we've got to crush this weapons trade!" Marcus slapped his desk. "Find the white men who're in on it. Tell me, Lieutenant." Marcus fixed the officer with a stare. "How do you suppose the Indians pay for guns?"

Hazelcrest shrugged. "Abduct women and children from settlements, sell them in Mexico for slaves. Ransom cattle that they stop on drives. Take gold and greenbacks they find when raiding, though redskins don't normally value money."

"You've the same ideas I do, Lieutenant. But the problem of doing something still remains."

There was a knock outside the office.

"Come in."

Phil Turnbo pushed open the door and saluted.

"Yes, Captain?" Marcus looked up attentively.

"You mentioned earlier calling at the hog ranch today, sir. The afternoon's getting along."

"You're right. It is." He idly scratched his mustache for a moment, then turned back to Hazelcrest. "Lieutenant, you've had a damned frustrating week out on the scout. I'll let you go now. Get cleaned up and take some rest. Thanks for the report. You're dismissed."

When they were alone, Marcus told Turnbo, "The hog ranch. Yes." He took his kepi from a wall peg and put on the jaunty hat. "It's time I met this Jack Kyle and talked to him. There've been no complaints about his saloon, but then, what soldier that I know would be likely to gripe? Not about a low-drinking place that runs whores. It comes to me to warn Kyle that I don't want him cheating my men — at least not too badly."

"Right, sir."

"Let's go."

Although the distance wasn't far, the commander had arranged to have his and the captain's horses brought around. It was just possible that Jack Kyle, saloon owner, was the kind inclined to scorn a major willing to walk to such a meeting. The purpose of the visit was to put Kyle in his place — whether things turned out cordial or not. It made sense to make a strong impression.

"Let's go, Champion," he breathed to the tall black gelding that was his favorite. The horse had been with him since his Fort Bowie days, and was deep-bottomed, strong-legged and fast.

Turnbo fell in alongside his superior, and the pair

trotted leisurely off the compound. They drew up in front of the main soddy of the hog ranch in just a few short minutes. Marcus and Turnbo swung down, tied their reins to the hitching rail and folded their gauntlets under their belts.

Shoving through the bat wings, Marcus took in the layout, the two bar areas with the partial wall separating them, the knot of tables for playing cards, the hallway to the rear and the curtained-off whores' lairs. The shutters of the large room were open, admitting sunshine, and the lanterns hanging from the ceiling weren't lit in the daytime.

As for patrons, there were no military men. This was natural, since duty hours were still in full swing. Several men and a quartet of tawdry females lounged about in chairs. Marcus picked the mustached fellow in the clean shirt as the famous Mr. Kyle. That left two civilian males with scrubby beards, the more ugly one wearing a frayed patch over his left eye. Both men were clad in buckskins and dark-colored slouch hats. The hats, by their condition, might have survived a stampede. But both men's clothes were filthy and tattered.

One additional woman, wearing a long skirt and not a provocative knee-length one like the whores, sat by herself at a baize-topped table against the rear wall. She shuffled a deck of cards aimlessly, not seeming to need the practice. She was a surprisingly fetching redhead.

That's got to be the one, Marcus thought. There were rumors linking her with young Nate Ambrose. The fascinating thing about gossip in the army was that it always reached the commanding officer sooner or later, without exception.

Marcus, with Turnbo following, bypassed the surly civilian drinkers. Each owned a personal bottle, and they occupied themselves with frequent swigs. Several empties lay on the packed-dirt floor. The officers strode toward the presumed owner.

"Mr. Jack Kyle?" Marcus said. "I'm Major Cavanaugh from the cantonment you rely on for protection. The commanding officer, in fact. I decided to stop by and meet you." He paused. "Oh, and you may already know Captain Turnbo. I believe you've had the pleasure of his presence here by now."

Jack Kyle preened his walrus mustache and fingered a cigar. "Pleased, I'm sure, Major. Yes, I've met the captain." He nodded and flashed a yellow smile. "Can I offer you gents — er, officers — drinks?"

"Not just now. It's a bit early. But I feel a conversation is in order."

"Well, in that case," Jack Kyle said, puffing his stogy, "there's tables standing around empty. Let's just set our tired asses down."

"Let me come to a point, Mr. Jack Kyle," Marcus said. "The reason you founded this establishment where you did is clear. You propose to make profits from sales to army men. The selling is of liquor and feminine flesh — "

"Er, may we say 'entertainment'?"

"You may. *I'll* call a spade a spade." Seated next to Marcus, Phil Turnbo squelched a grin.

"Now, Kyle," the major continued, "it's a free country, as they say, and places like this have always existed around military posts. There's even something to be said for meeting soldiers' needs. The ins and outs of that issue, though, aren't the reason for this chat. The reason is, mister, that any gambling that's done here, I want it clean. I want your beer and whiskey fairly priced and of wholesome quality. I can't have troopers in hospital from adulterated spirits."

"Now just hold on — "

"You know even better than I, Kyle, the kind of stuff that gets passed off as whiskey. Grain alcohol flavored with hot-pepper juice, or gunpowder, or worse. I don't want to learn such is served here."

"It ain't."

"I've no cause not to believe you today. Well, Mr. Kyle, I guess that covers the reason that I — "

A crash of furniture and breaking glass rang out. Kyle and the officers jumped up and whirled. Over near the bar, one of the tables had been turned over and the bottles upset and spilled. The two men in buckskins had the bartender by the arms, and they proceeded to run him hard into the packed-sod wall. The victim's balding head rammed the sod with a thud. A frightened squawk erupted from his mouth. The man with the eye patch began driving punches to his lower back. The bartender howled at the punishment to his kidneys. The second man drooled whiskey in his beard and laughed.

Marcus moved to interfere, but Jack Kyle was quicker. Dropping his cigar and stepping past the clutch of shrieking whores, the saloon-keeper snatched a bung starter from behind the bar and swung it to impact the roughhousing man's skull. The man sighed and collapsed. His partner started to rush Kyle, but stopped, frozen in his tracks.

Marcus glimpsed the tiny pistol that Jack Kyle held. The derringer fit nicely in the owner's hand and the threat it posed was backed by the mustached man's words. "Don't mix in this no more, Montooth!"

"But my pard, Finn, there, he — "

"Goddamn it, I said not to mix in!"

The man called Montooth swore under his breath and flexed his gnarled fingers as if he was anxious to wrap them around Kyle's throat. Meanwhile, the barman staggered to a tall cupboard, from which he pulled a shotgun. "Stand back, Jack," he hissed.

"You ain't ventilating nobody, Hutchins!"

"He called me a ball-less jackass,"Hutchins told his boss. "Hell, he called you a low sidewinder!"

"And maybe I am. You, Montooth," he snarled. "Call it settled?"

The man spat. "Oh, I reckon."

"Help your friend up."

Hauled back to his feet, Finn straightened his patch and put a hand to his battered head. A considerable lump had formed above his ear, and blood was smeared across his cheek. "Damn it, Kyle, what you do that for?"

"'T'ain't no time to be making trouble in this place." He pointed with his chin at the officers. Marcus noted the gesture.

Everyone suddenly seemed more relaxed. The soiled doves were back in their corner, huddled in low talk. But Retta Cantrell looked exactly as she had. The short-lived uproar had not distracted her from her solitary card handling.

Jack Kyle, not a hair out of place on his sleek head, was smiling genially at Marcus. "Major, let me apologize for the little dust-up. These things'll just happen sometimes, but we try and settle them as fast as we can. You notice no army men got hurt this time. I don't mean for any ever to."

"I'm sure," Marcus said. "Well, Captain Turnbo

and I had best be getting back."

"Yeah. Well, good luck to you both, Major, Captain. With your soldiering, or whatever."

When the officers were mounted again and trotting in the shade along the Sweetwater, Turnbo turned in the saddle. "Did you notice, Major, the restraint shown when that fight broke out? Kyle didn't force the troublemakers out. And they settled down rather promptly, considering."

"I noticed," the major replied. "And I can only say this. The whole bunch knew each other pretty well. Which is remarkable way out here, wouldn't you agree?" He heeled Champion in the flanks, and the eager black lifted to a lope. Phil Turnbo gave spur and followed.

Chapter Ten

A few days later, the arrival of an advance messenger at the cantonment gave the outpost an hour's notice of the approach of a column of men in dusty uniforms. There was a lot of snap and jangle in the demeanor of the wide-eyed noncoms, and the captain, with his plumed campaign hat and kidskin knee boots, was a model of a dashing escort commander. Even privates in the ranks rode with backs straighter than the army had the right to expect. They made a grand show crossing the parched parade ground of the Cantonment on the Sweetwater.

If the small outpost had been assigned a band, Marcus Cavanaugh would have turned them out with their instruments gleaming under the hot Texas sun. They'd have bleated some quick-step tune with clarinet and cornet flourishes. Such was the pomp and ceremony befitting the arrival of a brigadier general, particularly one of status in the army's department of Texas. But Marcus had done his best. He'd taken a shave and haircut from his dutiful striker, and had his dress uniform sponged, the brass buttons and insignia polished. His boots shone with fresh blacking. He wore his saber in its scabbard at his side.

He stood in front of headquarters, the Stars and Stripes on high, watching the important visitor from San Antonio dismount his dappled steed. General Cyrus Bingham was weighty in bulk as well as authority, but he heaved from the saddle with a nervous energy, waving his striker's help aside. In his late fifties, he wore his dense, cropped beard and his side whiskers like a badge of rich pewter gray. His face was red from sweating in the sun.

"General, welcome." Marcus stepped forward after saluting, Ambrose and Hazelrest flanking him.

"So, Major Cavanaugh. We meet again."

The man was right. The two had met, but that had been five years earlier at Camp Richardson. Bingham had been a colonel then, overbearing, a stickler for discipline, but with a genial streak as well. He was also overly proud of his son, Hayes, who at that time was a plebe at West Point.

Hayes Bingham, lieutenant of the United States Cavalry. Wounded by hostile Indians in the Texas panhandle, an arm and a leg amputated, June, 1875. Or had the shavetail been discharged by now, written off on disability? Marcus was willing to bet he'd not be kept waiting long to hear the outcome of that miserable affair.

"First let me give some orders to my aide, Major, and then I'd like a private talk with you in your office." Bright, pale eyes glittered above Bingham's fleshy cheeks, but the general looked somewhat unhealthy. It was as if he carried volcanoes of emotion inside, smoldering. Sorrow? Marcus wondered. Regret? Or anger? The commander of the cantonment waited patiently. Bingham spoke to a junior officer. The voices were soft. Marcus didn't strain his ears to overhear. "All ready," the general said finally.

"The headquarters is back over this way, General. By the way, repairs to the cantonment have gone along rather well. I believe we've finally got things whipped into shape."

"Indeed?"

Inside the roomy building of earthen brick, the major and the general went directly back to Cavanaugh's office. Although spartan as far as furniture went — a battered oak desk, a couple of storage cabinets, spindle chairs with arms — Marcus had tried to avert dreariness. A flag draped one wall and several maps hung opposite. Behind the desk, to the side of the lone window, were positioned mounted antelope prongs.

Cyrus Bingham dropped in a chair, loosened the top buttons of his officer's tunic and tossed his hat on the desk — arrogantly, in Marcus's view.

Seated himself, and leaning back behind the desk, Marcus asked politely, "Some liquid refreshment, General? The orderly can fetch cool tea. Or — "

"Let's get to the point of my coming all the way from San Antonio." Bingham crossed his plump legs and spoke in an abrasive, gruff voice. "This Llano Estacado is Texas's answer to the verge of hell. Fit for snakes and scorpions to frolic in, but a damned wasteland for human beings. The fact that our Comanche foes call it home proves the redskins aren't men really, but akin to the lesser beasts. Be that as it may. It's for two reasons mainly, Major Cavanaugh, that the policy of the War Department turns to clearing these parts of Indians. First, the savages based here have spread their raids over a wide area as far as the homesteaded lands up north and the cattle range down south. Intolerable killing of innocent settlers!"

"Two reasons, did you say, General?"

Bingham uncrossed his legs and glared. "The other has to do with safe travel lanes. Prosperity in south Texas depends on cattle reaching Kansas railheads. We're talking safety for those herds, Major. And we can expect more emigrant trains with the opening of the gold fields out to the west."

Marcus calmly stoked his brown-and-gray mustache. "I can see that well enough, General Bingham. Indeed, I receive directives and written orders on the subject almost by the bale. My small garrison here, despite undermanning, is charged with securing the wagon routes, giving aid when requested by buffalo-hunting expeditions, and seeking out and defeating hostile raiding parties. You've come a long way to deliver a familiar message, General. But I think I know why."

Bingham slapped his hand on his knee. "I'll state it flatly. The war leader Leaping Wolf and his band remain at large. You, Cavanaugh, have been unable to stop their raids, and scarcely a week passes without more Comanches jumping the reservations over in the Indian Territory. Our information is that these people are joining Leaping Wolf. A sizable population of hostiles is building, including women and children. And if it isn't stopped, the situation hereabouts will encourage Indians everywhere to take up murderous ways."

"Let me make a point or two myself?"

Bingham cleared his throat loudly. "Proceed."

"Well, for one thing, General," Marcus said, "if the tribes actually received all rations and supplies agreed to in treaties, they wouldn't be so easy to stir up. The second thing — and I've stated this often in written reports — Leaping Wolf is being supplied with brand-new rifles. Now, to bring that off, there have to be white men trafficking. Sir, I've been trying to find a way — "

"Aha!"

Marcus frowned. "Sir?"

"You've admitted the problem, Major. You've been trying, not succeeding! I've just traveled a lot of dusty miles to light a fire under you, your officers and all the men of this outpost. Before this summer is out, the army wants the uprising quelled. And my feeling, Cavanaugh, is that the answer's a campaign. Not patrols, but a campaign!"

Along the lane outside the building rode a group of troopers just breaking up a mounted drill. The trotting horses raised a gritty haze that crept in the window along with a chorus of noise. Marcus Cavanaugh sat with his features motionless, concealing his rising anger.

"It's been my judgment, General," he finally said, "that the kind of expedition you suggest would be foolish, given our numbers at this outpost. All we could do is take the companies out to look for cold trails and follow any we find — at least until they give out. Or the troops could be surprised by a superior force — an even worse occurrence. As long as Leaping Wolf keeps moving and never settles at a base, he's a will o' the wisp. Aside from being better armed than the army."

"Damn, Major! Then you're inclined to quarrel with my orders?"

Marcus's mouth was rigid. "I've heard no actual orders from you, General Bingham. I've heard only suggestions as to what the army wants. Not quite the same thing."

General Cyrus Bingham bristled. His gray beard twitched above the ropy veins in his neck, and his eyes flashed with venom. "You damn better take what I say as orders to you, Major," he hissed. "Combine your companies and get a squadron in the field before the month is out. Keeping to the outpost to avoid casualties is lollygagging. I want fire and sword wrought on those savages for what they've done! God damn them!"

"General, I know how you must feel about Lieutenant Bingham. But you want revenge for what happened to your son. Throwing away troopers' lives is not an answer. I've kept my men ready to march. They'd have done so at the first word from scouts as to where a decisive engagement might be fought. Or word about the rifle merchants, who make big profits at the expense of settlers' lives. Your son Hayes took a chance being away from his troops, General. He was unlucky. He was about as unlucky as a man can be. But at least he came out of it alive. Your son's not lost to you."

"The hell he isn't! He's half a man! Less than half a man! Not only without his right arm and left leg, but enslaved to laudanum, Cavanaugh! That damned opium! Do you know what my son's life amounts to now? He's either raving or he's asleep!" The general slumped back in his chair, and for a moment, covered his eyes with his hands. "Oh, my God. Oh, my God."

"I had no way of knowing about this last, sir."

Straightening suddenly, the anger coursed through his system again. Cyrus Bingham stared fiercely. "I don't care about casualties to C, D and F Companies Major Cavanaugh! I want Leaping Wolf's warriors slaughtered just as those savages slaughtered my hopes! And if I don't get what I want — "

Marcus waited.

"You won't get what you want, either, Cavanaugh! I assume you want to get ahead in this man's army! Not see future promotions blocked! Not find yourself posted to the most stagnant holes, to watch your career grow stagnant, too! Do you hear what I'm saying? Do you understand?"

The major nodded.

"Those companies in the field! Within the month! I'm heading back south after reveille in the morning, Major, along with my escort. But I'll be waiting in San Antonio to hear of results against Comanches! And if I don't . . ."

Bingham was on his feet and striding toward the door. In another second, he was through it. Mounted troopers clattered past outside. Now it was Marcus Cavanaugh's turn to slump in his chair. It was shaping up to be a hard summer — and one that would be bloody, too.

Chapter Eleven

Deep in Indian Territory, and far from the Cantonment on the Sweetwater, Gloriana Hollister awaited her husband quietly in a glade at the base of the tall canyon wall. It was pleasant under the trees, less abominably smelly than her dwelling, and less hot. She busied her hands plaiting her waist-length chestnut hair, aware of the cooking and other chores she was neglecting. She didn't care, even though her husband would be displeased when he returned from gambling with his friends. Despondent, her will to survive seemed harder to maintain each day. It had reached the point where she simply no longer cared. Her thoughts drifted to the hateful other woman in her husband's life.

Sometimes Gloriana was confused as to who was the favorite. True, the other woman was tougher and stronger, and having been married to him longer had borne him a son. But it was to Gloriana he came to vent his violent lust. Those were the times she loathed most. She had learned to shut her mind off at the backbreaking drudgery of life in the camp. She didn't even think about the past, her life before her capture. The time when her real family was alive and happy on the Kansas homestead. The time before the awful slaughter the Comanche raiders had wrought.

Gloriana heard Leaping Wolf's first wife call from beyond the tipi, a disgusting gutteral sound. But she wasn't going to answer to Rushing Water Woman. She scooted further under the leafy shrubs that lined the bottom of the great, deep canyon where the Indian encampment lay. The deerskin dress that she wore protected her skin from brambles, for which she was grateful. A cloth frock would have been torn to shreds. She prayed that Leaping Wolf might seek her elsewhere, but she had no such luck.

"Moon Dove Woman!" He called out the damnable name the Indians had given her. Leaping Wolf was nearby and striding closer. The haughty figure of the renowned war leader strode past the tipi and into full view. Atop powerful shoulders, Leaping Wolf had a block head, with high cheekbones, sinister slits for eyes, and his downturned mouth was like a lipless gash. Raven-black hair fell in fat braids down the front of his massive chest. The Indian's wrists, where his buckskin sleeves ended, were thick as most men's arms. In his powerful hands, he clutched two half-cured human scalps.

He saw the tracks that she'd left and came straight to her hiding place. A powerful hand wrenched Gloriana to her feet. Leaping Wolf's glittering eyes impaled the young woman. "Here are the trophies of my slain enemies!" He was very angry. "These should be smoking on the rack before the fire. But the fire has gone out. What does Moon Dove Woman have to say?"

"I did not know the fire had gone out." She could speak Comanche only haltingly.

"You should have been tending it." The war leader thrust his fierce face close to her. She smelled pungent sweat and the rancid flesh clinging to the scalps. "And there is the skin of the deer that I shot. Rushing Water Woman works alone to scrape the fat and hair. It is for Moon Dove Woman to gather fuel, scrape hides, stitch the tipi."

Gloriana didn't speak.

Leaping Wolf scowled. "You are insolent. You must obey your husband."

In the sycamore's cool shade, she shrugged.

"You must be punished. Let it take place now by my hand. Pull your dress over your head, Moon Dove Woman." The warrior's voice had grown still more harsh. "Bend yourself from the waist and put your hands on the sapling trunk!"

She felt as helpless as a bird stalked by a snake. She found herself obeying automatically. Naked and exposed, she quaked with fright. When he brought up his thong riding quirt behind her, she heard its sibilant swish. The strands lashed her tender rump. She refused to cry out.

Leaping Wolf plied the thong again and again, not with the full great strength of his arm, but with strokes appropriately restrained. This wasn't a foe that he chastised, but his foolish, lazy second wife. She was young, and a white captive, taken just recently. He remembered fondly the raid on the homestead. This one young woman with the pale face and brown hair had fascinated him. He'd brought her back to the village hidden in the canyon to possess her for his own. When her buttocks were crisscrossed with welts, Leaping Wolf stilled his arm. "Moon Dove Woman, I have finished your whipping."

She held her head down still. Tears welled in her sky-blue eyes.

"But Leaping Wolf is not through!" He grabbed her and yanked her to him roughly. He fumbled at his leggings. He opened his garment and he forced her down, stretching her on the ground. Then he dropped on her and wrenched her legs apart. He penetrated and thrust violently. His foul breath disgusted her. His oily face shone with ravening lust. She felt her body would burst. Gloriana Hollister vented a scream.

In the darkness of the lean-to, Nate Ambrose humped and bucked and pumped his seed. Retta Cantrell squirmed her own pleasure. The partners rolled apart, exhausted, and lay atop the blanket on the cot. Gradually, Ambrose's heartbeat returned to normal, and then his senses. He felt the scratch of the straw tick on his cheek, the flow of sweat down his back.

The pair lay staring at the black ceiling for a long, long time. Faintly the bugle call taps filtered from the cantonment. It meant lights out for all the soldiers. The lieutenant laughed. It had been lights out in this place for over an hour.

He was about to say something, but the woman sensed it and put a finger to his lips. He felt the coolness of her slender hand. He spoke anyway. "I want to tell you — "

"I have the feeling you're going to say what you

tried to say before," Retta said. "You're with me now and think it's fine, but I don't want you to count on its being permanent. Don't think about the future at all. I don't. Oh, I just don't know if you can understand."

"I'll try." He shifted his weight, reached to touch her, found that in the darkness, she'd swung long bare legs to the floor and sat erect. "I understand this much," he mumbled. "There seems to be something in your past."

"Uh-huh."

"Yet I know you're not like the other women at this hog ranch. It isn't your way to go with men for the money, nor has it ever been. You're a decent sort, Retta. Only, strangely, involved with Jack Kyle."

"To run the gambling end of the establishment. To earn some money. Get a stake together to — "

"Go to San Francisco. You told me that. Why won't you accept my own offer as a great improvement on that plan?"

A sigh. "I guess I'm not the marrying kind, Nate."

"Damn!"

In the ensuing quiet, she struck a sulfur match and lit a candle. The golden flame's glow showed her skin pale and smooth as ivory. She then proceeded to light a short, pencil-thin cigar.

"I don't want you staying in this place, Retta," Nate Ambrose said. "Having to associate with the men that come in, you know? The customers. Or see the things that go on, and be involved in them. That poker table of yours is no island."

She smiled faintly. "You find the troopers a wicked bunch? Is that it?"

"By the look of other types passing this way, the troopers seem angels. What about that pair in the filthy buckskins, the ones who stink of rotten meat and old blood?"

"Finn and Montooth? They cleared out days ago, Nate."

"This trip. They were here before, and I expect them to come through again. They're damned cozy with the boss, Kyle."

Retta Cantrell exhaled smoke. "They're stupid buffalo hunters, that's all. You've seen the fleabag mules and wagons that they travel in. They say combing the plain for buffs isn't what it used to be. Not many of the animals left. High prices back east for hides, though. That's the only thing that keeps them in the game."

"Sounds fishy."

She shrugged. "They're just looking for the phantom Red River herd."

"You never knew them before?"

"No."

"I believe you. I believe you because I like you. But now I have to go."

"The army."

"I'm supposed to be in quarters. If there's trouble, and I''m not there, well — "

"It would mean good-bye to your precious career. I catch the drift."

"If we two were to get married — "

She shook her red head firmly. "That can't be, Nate."

"Damn!"

But as he swore, he was also pulling on his clothes. He buttoned his tunic with the stiff officer's shoulder boards and adjusted his kepi. "I won't see you till I'm back from my next patrol. D Company rides out in the morning."

"Until I see you, then," she said.

Irritated, he left without kissing her. Later, in his bachelor's bed, he wished he had.

"The general's gone, so let's get down to business, Sergeant Keogh. Send for Gilliam."

The early morning's rays flooded in the headquarters. "Yes, sir! Right away, sir!"

"I'll meet him at the shed. He's to act as interpreter, which Swift Deer expects. And, of course, the other that I told the scout last night."

Marcus Cavanaugh jammed his kepi on and walked into the full sunlight, squinting across the parade. D Company was moving off the post, Nate Ambrose at the head of the snaking column. At the tail, eating dust, a half-dozen pack mules plodded. The troopers themselves would rotate positions on the march, some eating dust one day, others the next. But the packers always plodded last. Carried at the head of the troop, the guidon pennant spanked bravely against the bright blue Texas sky.

With luck, the troops would also have a chance to be brave. Marcus watched them file out, then turned along the path. Keogh had assembled guards and posted at attention. Gilliam came up in his characteristic lope. "We won't waste time with this," Marcus snapped. " Unbar the door."

This was done, and the Comanche was prodded out by a couple of privates. He'd lost a little weight and the graze on his brow had scabbed over. His black eyes were dull. Swift Deer's smell had grown worse, too, Marcus decided, standing downwind. The major edged around to the Indian's left and noted the knots in the ropes that held his wrists tightly.

"Ask him again who sells his tribesmen guns."

The gutteral sounds that Gilliam spoke were curt. Maybe there were some insults thrown in. Swift Deer's nostrils flared, and he shook his big head haughtily. He was as tough as they came among Indians. There'd been several interrogations since the first attempt, and they'd all been fruitless. Swift Deer would let himself be killed before he'd give the information to betray his band. Torture would be no use. Comanche warriors were hardened by their painful manhood rituals.

Marcus stalked up to the bound but still-defiant Indian and raised his hand to strike the copper face. Swift Deer didn't flinch. Marcus lowered his arm.

"All right, turn him loose," he barked. "Tell him, Gilliam, that he'll be given the pony that he rode when taken. That it's been in the corral all this time. That he can go and return to Leaping Wolf's camp, and tell the war leader of the blue-coats' warning that the raiders must surrender. If they do so now, before more harm is done, they can go on reservations. If they refuse, they'll be hunted down and killed. Tell Swift Deer that the choice is Leaping Wolf's. And that the war leader must make it soon."

Marcus turned on his heel and walked off, passing the dun pony that was being led up by a stable hand. A trooper slashed the bonds from the captive's wrists. If Swift Deer was startled by the quick change in his fortune he gave no sign. At a gesture from Gilliam and a flood of words, he moved cautiously to the skittish pony. When he saw no guns pointed at him, he came to life, vaulted to his mount's back, trotted a few yards, then paused to look back.

Still no threatening moves were made. Marcus lifted his hand again, a wave. Only open ground lay between them and the trees and creek and the edge of the cantonment. Swift Deer wheeled the pony about and kicked it to a gallop. Quickly he left the compound behind and cantered west across the plain.

When the Comanche was a distant speck, a hostler led Sabine Gilliam's strong roan out. The scout leaped to the saddle and slapped his booted rifle. The saddlebags were filled with food and canteens.

"Now don't follow too close," Marcus called needlessly. The plan had been carefully laid, and the scout knew it well. "The groove the blacksmith filed in the pony's hoof will make the right trail clear."

"Major, I'll do them things!" Sabine Gilliam gave spur and the roan burst into motion.

Marcus watched his best hope of bringing the Comanches to heel ride across the yard. "There he goes, Captain," he said to Turnbo, beside him. "Let's all keep our fingers crossed."

Chapter Twelve

Sabine Gilliam rode across the windswept plain. The deep-vee notch in the rear hoof of Swift Deer's pony — the work of the cantonment blacksmith — had made the mount visible for any tracker who possessed the skill. And Gilliam, the half-Delaware breed, was one of the best sign readers in the army's staff of contract scouts.

He'd served with General Crook's Dakota campaign at Smoky Hill River, and with Colonel Mac-Kenzie at his defeat of the Kotsotekas at McClellan Creek. Together with Yellowstone Kelly and the legendary Grouard, at one time, he'd even worked for Colonel Custer. But he'd disliked the brevet "boy general's" arrogance, and moved back down to Texas for a change of scene.

Now he served the Cantonment on the Sweet-water, a civilian with a contract to guide, interpret and, when required, even acting as emergency courier. "Congenial employment, most often leading to a terrible death" were Custer's words describing a scout's job. There was truth to it, too, as well as a clever ring. But Sabine Gilliam was a man determined to stay alive.

Some called him as devious as a coyote, and others said he was as brave as a lynx. He himself made no such comparisons. He was just a man out to do a job, and incidentally, survive. On this mission he kept well back of Swift Deer throughout the day, not wanting to be spotted. As the long day wound down, the setting sun colored and turned gaudy. Bands of magenta-tinged clouds blended with rose and mauve hues, then the orange disk was floating in a sky of brass. The occasional sagebrush that Gilliam rode past threw enormous shadows. The sun sank finally, and evening silence ruled the land.

There would be no moonrise for hours, so Sabine Gilliam set himself a cold, dry camp. Parched corn and jerky — not ration hardtack — made his meal, and he washed the food down with canteen water. He unsaddled, but left the saddle packed and tied, ready to toss on the roan's back in a hurry. The horse was picketed. He stretched himself out on the hard flat ground, and was asleep almost immediately.

He woke at the first bird call, and rolled to his feet, fully booted and clothed. He scanned the 360-degree view keenly in the dusky predawn gray. He caught sight of a jack rabbit and a far-off pronghorn, but today wasn't for hunting. Swift Deer was nowhere in sight.

Sabine Gilliam saddled up and mounted. Only when he was trotting rapidly toward the west did he take time to eat, and then betook himself of the same cured jerky as before. As the new morning grew light, he could see the marked hoofprints that he followed better. He kept the same slow, steady pace across the parched grassland. The character of the terrain changed subtly as the sun climbed the vacant sky to noon zenith.

The landscape became gently serrated, the flat plains giving way to rows of long, uneven hills. But the slopes were thickly grassed, and there were more clumps of sage. Runty pin oaks appeared in the depressions, and a scattering of cedars as well. There were even occasional small streams.

Still, Sabine Gilliam pressed the roan that he straddled, mile after endless mile. He lunched, again on dry traveler's food, dismounting to drink at one of the trickling rills. The roan cropped grass during the rest period, until Gilliam heaved aboard and hit the trail again.

Gilliam saw the dun horse lying on the ground a long way off, and reined up sharply. A thorough scan ahead with his field glasses showed the animal was dead. He saw no Swift Deer about, however. The dun pony had apparently given out, and its rider had gone on afoot. A lone Comanche's moccasin tracks in dry grass would be harder to dog than the dun-marked hoof, but he could do it. The man would be traveling very slowly, after all. The main risk now would be not to overtake Swift Deer, or fall victim to ambush.

The sudden attack seemed to come straight out of the blue. From near at hand, a stone slammed the roan mount's nose. Spooked, the animal kicked and reared. As the rider fought to stay in the saddle, he glimpsed another deadlier threat. From behind a hummock, the big red devil, Swift Deer, charged out on foot. He had no weapons but his hands, but he moved with fierce desperation. The copper-dark face was a mask of hate.

Despite weeks of confinement in the army post's tool shed, the warrior was still formidably strong. He grabbed Gilliam's leg and jerked it from the stirrup. The scout toppled from his horse. He landed on the ground with an impact that jarred the wind from his lungs. The warrior dropped on him with both knees, one to the vulnerable solar plexus. Pinwheels of pain lanced through Gilliam. He felt himself pounded with hard fists, and then hands wrapped around his neck tightly.

The stranglehold cut off his breathing. Gilliam bucked and pitched in an attempt to fling his enemy off, but failed. The flow of blood to his brain slowed and his sight dimmed. His tongue burst between his lips. With a mighty effort of will, Gilliam managed to wrench his struggling frame a last time, hooking a knee under the Comanche's chin. Now the two adversaries rolled on the ground together, kicking and punching. Gilliam jammed a solid knee into Swift Deer's groin.

The Comanche roared with pain, and flopped violently backward. Sabine Gilliam bolted upright, and saw Swift Deer come to his feet as well. Gilliam's Bowie knife was in Swift Deer's fist. The Comanche darted, leading viciously with the blade. Gilliam's sleeve parted and a slit opened in his forearm from wrist to elbow. Swift Deer rushed in and slashed again, slicing only air. The scout pitched sidelong from his path.

"*Aaaaah!*" the savage roared. The cords in his arms twitched like banjo strings.

Gilliam's hand flashed to his holster, dipped, then

came up with his Colt. He cocked the six-gun and fired in a single, lightning move. The .45 boomed and the bullet pierced the Comanche's neck. A flood of crimson blood burst from the wound, and from Swift Dear's screaming mouth. Gilliam fired again and blew his foe's eye into the center of his skull.

Swift Deer toppled like an exploded chimney and lay quite motionless in the grass. He had to be dead, but Sabine Gilliam took no chances. This had been one of the closest calls in a life that had seen many fights and battles. After minutes passed, he toed the still form and peered in its face. A whitish film had formed over the one intact eye, and a cloud of flies had already gathered in the hideous empty socket.

The lister bucket hit the barracks wall with a tinny crash, rebounded and rattled along the floor, finally rolling to a stop. Private Ike Kendall flung himself between the row of bunks in the direction of his enemy. Cobb Orly grinned wickedly, balled his fists into bony bludgeons and awaited his chance to swing.

"Goddamn your hide!" The squat, stocky man laughed. He spat on the floor through brown teeth. "Come an' get it, beanpole! Call me a thief — you got to back your play! And you ain't shit with your fists! I'm gonna bust that ugly puss o' yorn!"

In the hush of the deserted dormitory, the raucous voices echoed. It was the hour for the troopers to be at mess. Now was the time to settle differences in the large deserted room. Only this wasn't a mere difference of opinion, but a difference between two sharply distinct breeds of men. Kendall the farm boy had

97

come a long way in the few months since he'd enlisted. He could march and do a presentable manual of arms. He'd ridden patrols led by Captain Turnbo, and sniffed the danger of nearby hostiles in the prairie wind.

It was time to stop getting pushed around by Orly, he felt. Orly was an old military hand who'd served many enlistments, not all under the same name. But he was lazy, a coward, a liar and he had a nasty mean streak. And now he was a thief.

By accident, Ike Kendall had caught his foe red-handed. When Kendall had strolled in, Cobb Orly had been rifling through Kendall's rucksack. Now the evidence was wrapped around the thick neck of the short man — a new red bandanna that Kendall had bought with his hard-earned pay, all ten cents' worth. The sutler's asking price had been high, but there were no issue bandanas to be had on post. And now Kendall's prize possession was tied on Orly's neck!

"Here I come, Orly!" The skinny man charged, his toothpick arms flailing.

"Stop it, you men! Stop that!" yelled Sergeant Hoffman, who suddenly filled the doorway. "There'll be no fighting in the barracks!"

Kendall sledged a blow to Orly's body that stunned him, but the veteran recovered quickly. He lashed out and booted Kendall's knee. Kendall staggered but wouldn't fall. He brought an elbow around to jab the side of Orly's head. Orly, propelled backward, tripped and sprawled across a bed, making it collapse.

"Private, Goddamn it!" Hoffman rushed into the fray. Orly flung a broken bedpost. Missing Kendall, it struck the sergeant in his chest. He grunted in surprise and pain.

"Now you gone an' done it," Kendall whooped. "Mind, Orly, you'd best turn the bandanna over! You're plumb whupped!"

"Shit!"

"Thievin' bastard! Take this!"

Heinrich Hoffman was shouting at the top of his lungs: "Troopers! In here! Stop the fight!" Through the doorway surged a blue tide. Several privates and a couple of corporals piled onto Orly and Kendall using knees, fists and whatever else came to hand. Within minutes, the first combatants had their arms pinned to their sides. "To the top sergeant, boys," the German-born noncom ordered. His blouse was ripped and he'd lost a button. His mood was far fouler than a minute before, because he hated to sew.

Ten minutes later, the wrongdoers stood at attention in the orderly room, bruised faces, torn uniforms and all. Patrick Keogh's bloodshot eyes raked the pair with scorn. He reached out a chevroned arm and plucked the bandanna from Cobb Orly's throat. "T'was this, then, the cause of it? The fracas? And t'ain't even a regulation scarf? Hell, you say!"

Major Cavanaugh stalked into the room. "I'll be with Lieutenant Hazelcrest over at the paddock, Keogh," he began. Seeing the two disheveled men, he paused. "What's this? Some trouble here with these troopers?"

"Brawling in the barracks, Major. It appears Orly here went and stole from the other man."

"Prescribe fitting punishment, Sergeant, if you please. Carry on."

Keogh knew Marcus Cavanaugh's usual policies regarding petty theft. "Orly, you'll do marchin' with a full backpack loaded with stones. All day. Three days. A lesson for all the other men with thievin' inclination."

Under his breath, Orly cursed.

"Startin' tomorrow! And tonight ye'll reside in the tight new guardhouse! Case closed!"

Just outside the building, Marcus found himself intercepted. Sabine Gilliam's roan trotted onto the parade and toward headquarters, a tired and hungry scout slouching in the saddle. The scout's left arm hung at his side, and his buckskins were stained. The swarthy face was grim.

"Gilliam!"

"Major. Yeah, I'm back. I had to kill the Comanche out there on the plain."

"Swift Deer? Before he led you to Leaping Wolf's camp?"

"That's about it."

Marcus, at that moment at least, was the most disappointed major on the frontier. He frowned. "Well, what's done is done. You had to save yourself, I can see. The only regret is that one bit of tracking seemed the best chance we had to locate the savages."

From the east, Phil Turnbo gigged his tall bay toward them in a canter. The officer reined up.

"What is it, Captain?" Marcus queried.

"Well, whether it's for good or for bad, only time will tell," Turnbo said. "We'll be getting company and soon. Oh, not Comanches this time. There's an emigrant train of wagons, a big one, heading our way. I've had Long Jaw Phelps's report, and I've ridden out and looked the outfit over myself. The shebang will be here by nightfall, I've no doubt."

"And the number of wagons?"

Turnbo considered. "Twenty. Twenty-five. Plenty

of women, old folks, children, Major. A real picnic. And the wagon boss? The famous Sam Adler, none else!"

Marcus frowned. "I've heard of Adler, even met him once at Sill. He built a reputation, all right. As a hothead and a brawler. Quick with his pistol, they say, and too willing to use it. This matter could require tact."

Turnbo laughed. "Tact, so the train will move on in a hurry, Major? I don't reckon that it's in the cards, not this trip. Their horses need a rest, and their equipment needs repair. And the would-be settlers are about exhausted. Give them at least a week in our neighborhood."

"A week?"

"Sure as we both went to West Point, Major!"

Chapter Thirteen

"Mr. Adler, good afternoon to you. Welcome to the cantonment."

Major Cavanaugh carefully sized up the man who stood before him. The late afternoon sun was low on the horizon, and the buildings cast long rectangular shadows. Sam Adler's face took on a blood-red tinge in the fading light. Despite a week's growth of whiskers, the wagon boss's features were sharply etched. It was the face of a man in his mid-thirties who'd ridden dangerous trails for a long time. Stubborn lines perched above the bridge of his hawk nose, and his eyes were like little holes scorched into rawhide.

"Major Cavanaugh? Well, howdy." Adler waited patiently for the man who was accompanying him to catch up. The individual was elderly as well as fat, and it was clear why he couldn't keep pace crossing the yard. He looked exhausted. The fringe of hair under his slouch hat was scanty, and his hand shook as he extended it to be shaken. Marcus obliged.

"Meet Ezra Chandler, Major," Adler said. "The Reverend Chandler, a real fire-and-brimstone preacher when he ain't plowing a field. Organizer of the train at its starting point, St. Joe. He's been feeling peaked lately, but the spirit remains. Ezra, this here's Major Cavanaugh."

"Reverend," Marcus acknowledged.

"Praise the Lord, Major Cavanaugh," Ezra Chandler said. "We in the train have reached a far point on our long, long journey. What Mr. Adler says is true: I've been a farmer all my life, not a traveler. But the land's used up back in Ohio, no more chance for a man there. The spirit came to me saying to head out west. And here me and my family members are — two sons and their wives and all the children they've had. And our bunch picked up still more members in Missouri — strangers then, but all fine folk. We're eighteen prairie schooners in all, Major. And when we find the land we want, we'll settle and raise us some crops."

"It's a grand idea, Reverend Chandler," Marcus said. "I'm afraid you have a way to go, though. The rainfall in these parts pretty much inhibits agriculture. I've seen the vegetables that our trooper gardeners raise, and they're rather stunted."

"Ah, irrigation may be the key then, my boy! We'll talk again on the subject when I'm rested more. These long days . . ." The resonant but weak old voice trailed off.

Marcus's gaze roamed past the two men and the buildings to the open land that stretched downstream along Sweetwater Creek. The big wagons and their teams rolled through a pall of yellow dust. One by one the bonneted Studebakers came to a stop in a planned formation. The train used much the same formation as a military squadron's supply wagons — a giant circle of vehicles abutting end to end. It offered the most protection against Indian raiders. Emigrants learned it fast or perished. The men on the seats bullied the laboring horses, some clearly more skilled than others. But the horses were tired, and the people were tired. Soon each wagon was put in place and the animals unhitched. Draft animals were corralled in the middle, near where the people ate and rested.

"Major," Chandler grunted, "I got to be gettin' back to my kin. I thank you on behalf of all of us for the protection and hospitality. All the folks'll be sleeping better whilst we're nigh the fort."

"Well, I'm glad to have met your acquaintance, Reverend."

"Me'n my wife Charity'd be honored by your presence at the camp later, Major, to meet some of the folks, share good coffee and just a bit of friendly talk. Our group's seen no new faces in many a week, and we're all anxious to show gratitude. Bring your other officers along, if they're willing. We'll do our best to be right sociable."

"Our pleasure, Reverend." Soldiers at an outpost needed change occasionally as well. Marcus planned to rope Hazelcrest and Turnbo into the occasion. Lieutenant Ambrose was with his company on patrol.

Chandler trudged off, but Sam Adler lingered in the dusk. With his hands on his waist above a businesslike gunbelt, he surveyed the outpost. "Not a big fort for way out here," the wagonmaster observed. "Got the Comanche buffaloed, have you, Major? Or have they got a mite many for you?"

Marcus appraised the wagonmaster coolly. "It's common knowledge that hostiles roam this country, Mr. Adler. Kiowas, and yes, Comanches. It's why they call it Comancheria. We've seen trouble from a war chief named Leaping Wolf who hates whites, too — and I mean massacre trouble. He leads a band that's well-armed with repeating rifles. He wiped out a wagon train last month, east of here. Beware, Mr. Adler, when you push on with those wagons you've been hired to guide."

The thickening shadows of night almost concealed Adler's face. When he smiled, though, a gleaming row of white teeth shone. A soft chuckle rumbled in his throat. "Glad you're willing to be plumb frank, Major. So many cavalry fellers ain't, and'll claim they got the Injuns on the run. I know a rough territory to cross when I see it, and I seen it today. I'll be keeping my eyes peeled, right enough."

"Maybe now you'll be frank with me," Marcus said. "Why did you pick this particular route west? You're supposed to be a sound wagonmaster. You've been taking these settler trains for years. Surely the Santa Fe Trail north of Dodge would have been a safer route."

"Money, Cavanaugh. Am I being frank enough? Chandler got him a late start in the year, but he wants Arizona Territory bad. Read about the gold fields in the newspapers. Aims to make good, same time as he brings the word to the sinning miners." His hand drifted to stroke his holstered Colt, then he went on. "He figures miners got to eat, and farms near mining camps are likely to pay off. The reverend upped the ante he's paying me to get him a quick trip.

To me, it's worth the risk."

"Are the men in the train armed and able-bodied?"

"You bet. But I didn't know 'bout them Comanches' new guns, I got to confess." The wagonmaster shrugged. "Oh, well. Now you have yourself a time at that campfire shindig, Major."

"I suppose I'll see you there."

"Hell, no." In the deep dusk, his grin flashed again. "I seen that hog ranch squatting beside this post of yours, Major. Reckon I'll wet my whistler some. Wash the dust out of a throat gone dry as old buffalo chips."

Marcus and Hazelcrest walked along the starlit path toward the wagon encampment. A number of fires glowed in the darkness, cooking the evening meal. As they approached, the officers saw the settlers, more men, women and children than could be readily counted. A concertina played a little jig amid the low buzz of excited talk.

Hazelcrest, though an older man and dour, was as fit for the occasion as Marcus Cavanaugh. Parties weren't the major's strongest enthusiasms, though he was sociable in conversation and liked people. The monthly balls and cotillions staged at Sill and Leavenworth bored him. He enjoyed women, not dancing, and his taste in music favored band marches or such songs as "Aura Lee" — if sentimental, then only mildly so. He'd attended enough grand waltzes and schottisches at West Point to last him a lifetime.

The ladies, however, liked to dress up when there was an excuse for it. And a beautiful woman turned out in a gown was a beguiling spectacle, to him as much as any man. Since this wasn't West Point or

Washington, but an outdoor camp at the edge of Texas' Llano Estacado, Marcus wasn't concerned that the evening would be other than amiable and plain. Now he and Hazelcrest squeezed their bodies through gaps between the wagons and found themselves in the midst of a small crowd. The people who gathered around them were excited and friendly.

"Glad you could make it," called a jolly male voice.

"You're as welcome as can be," rasped an old woman in a shawl.

"Lordy, ma, but they be handsome officers." This was a girl in her teens, awestruck at the sight of the two officers in their blue cavalry uniforms.

Ezra Chandler elbowed his way through the crowd. "Major Cavanaugh, a pleasure. And this is the only officer besides yourself on the post?"

Marcus introduced Hazelcrest, explained that Lieutenant Ambrose was out leading a patrol and Captain Turnbo was that day's duty officer. By then a woman nearly as stout as the reverend had moved to his side.

"Gentlemen, my wife, Charity. An excellent helpmeet and woman!"

"Pleased to meet you, ma'am."

"Yes, pleased."

She seemed to purr like the cat that got the cream at the attentions of the officers. Her gray curls bobbed and her plump fingers smoothed her apron. More introductions followed, to Dexter, Henry and Abraham Chandler, the preacher's sons, the youngest of whom had been named for the martyred president. All had wives, plain-looking farm women, and their young children flocked about.

Marcus filed the men's identities in his mind for

107

future reference, and tried to remember the women's names so as not to make a fool of himself before the night was out. The younkers he promptly forgot. He was an intelligent man, but confusion tended to set in with so many look-alike freckled, childish faces. Several other men of varying ages sauntered over, their spouses in tow, and the officers' conversational powers were again taxed.

Sam Adler was absent, as he'd said he would be. Marcus presumed that by now he confronted a whiskey glass over at Jack Kyle's bar. Or maybe a bottle. Marcus accepted a slice of pie, baked from dried peaches that evening in a Dutch oven buried in campfire coals. He glanced up and almost dropped his pewter fork. A woman whom he hadn't yet met was standing near him. Her willowy form was set off well in a plain dark dimity dress. Her light-brown hair created the illusion of a halo encircling her striking face. Lips, shaped like a Cupid's bow, curved in a shy smile.

The woman was tall, though not so tall as Marcus, and had a thin, female figure. She closed the distance between them in two steps and offered a shapely hand. "I want to thank you, too, Major. I'm Virginia Keel. And no, I don't hail from the Old Dominion state."

She's witty as well as pretty, Marcus Cavanaugh thought, sizing her up more closely in the firelight. "Pleased to meet you," he announced finally. "Would I have met your husband in the last few minutes, ma'am? I don't happen to recall — "

"My husband, Luke, is dead," she murmured. "He died on this journey, crossing the Canadian River after a storm. The high waters carried him away."

He studied Virginia Keel's good features still more carefully. She bore her tragedy with remarkable courage. "Mrs. Keel," he said solemnly, "I'm sorry to hear that."

In the noisy saloon soddy, hazy with smoke, it was difficult to hear, see or breathe. The voices of dozens of drunk cavalry troopers bounced off the walls. The carousing was intense because the bugled call to quarters would be coming all too soon, forcing the soldiers to plod back to the barracks, and flop for yet another uncomfortable night on their hard, bug-ridden bunks.

But for the moment at least, the evening was still young. Crack-skull whiskey could wet a thirsty gullet as long as a trooper's money lasted. Jack Kyle's glitter gals plied their trade casually, circulating among the men, begging for drinks, acting as tawdry decoration and receiving attention as such. Occasionally, a man would drift down the hall with one of the whores. It wasn't payday, so business wasn't that good, and no man had to wait his turn for very long.

Private Gib Franklin swigged an uncorked bottle, swallowed his plug-cut chaw by mistake and puked in a spittoon. Corporal Tim O'Malley guided the gal they called Snag-Tooth Ann into a crib. Creaks and groans erupted a minute later. Sergeant Neal called for one card in the game of draw poker that he was sitting in on. A pair of queens and a pair of deuces left some room for improvement. He suspected Sergeant Fritz Spitz held three of a kind at least. The foreign-born noncom had bid the pot up over a dollar for the first time all night.

"The gent with the chevrons takes a card, and the dealer takes two," Retta Cantrell murmured. Her slim fingers handled the squared pieces of pasteboard with customary ease. With the dealing complete, she set the deck down and fanned her own hand out to view it.

Only her practiced poker face concealed her pleasant surprise. She'd managed to fill an inside straight honestly. She well understood the theory of cheating, but she hated the practice. She tossed her red curls, and shoved a quarter across the baize. "Raise you boys twenty-five. Any challengers?"

The saloon's bat wings were flung wide, and the hard eyes of the man who stood there impaled her, drawing her glance like irresistible magnets. She felt a shiver race up and down her spine, and barely concealed an involuntary gasp. As the other players in the game tossed their cards down, defeated, she raked her in winnings. "Sorry, soldiers, but I'll be closing down for now. Try me tomorrow, won't you?" She forced a smile. The troopers grudgingly rose and left. The stocky civilian who had just entered strolled across the saloon toward her like a fox stalking a helpless chick. Finally he stood across the table from her, arms akimbo, his eyes narrowed and his mouth taunting.

"Retta," Sam Adler growled. "You? In this godforsaken hole?"

She dropped her gaze to the table for only the slightest moment before raising her head. Her face blanched chalk-white. "S-Sam?"

"What I'm going to do next, Retta, is sashay on out and around the back of the place." His tone was icy. "In a few minutes, you follow me. 'Cause, gal, I ain't partial to coming back in here and fetching you."

A few moments later, she found him outside in the same shadowy corner that she'd shared with Ambrose some nights earlier. There was no starlight this time, however. Even the moon lay hidden behind a screen of scudding clouds. The wagonmaster grabbed her and jerked her to him roughly.

"It's been quite a spell, ain't it, Retta?" Sam Adler growled. "I reckon you got a room and a bed hereabouts?"

"No!"

He squeezed her arm until fiery pain lanced her body.

"Yes! Yes! I have a small room!" she squealed.

"Let's go!"

With her face bleak and her steps dragging, she miserably led the way.

The guardhouse no longer had a guard — or at least, that was the way Cobb Orly saw it. It was quieter than hell in the coffin-dark confines of the tiny cell, and also quiet out beyond the single barred window. The prisoner had heard the scuffling of a soldier's boots hours earlier, before they'd passed him grub.

Now it had been night for a long time, and Cobb Orly felt bitter and bad. Bad because of his punishment for stealing Kendall's neckerchief. Bad about the army. Bitter over his whole wayfaring life. As he paced the cell, all his poor luck rose to mind, the bungled bank holdup at the age of sixteen, being jailed for four years. Rustling cows in the Rio Grande brakes and succeeding, only to get cheated by his pards. His first army enlistment was another disaster.

He'd fled hard Sioux fire in an engagement on the Cimarron, been cashiered and wound up deserting.

He'd taken a beating from a fancy man in Denver, and slit the fellow's whore's throat to get even. Then he was on the dodge again. And next back in the army in this miserable Texas hole. He was eating regularly, true, but working harder than ever in his life. And now they'd locked him up!

Anger rose in his throat like acid bile, and he threw himself against the wall. The earth bricks they'd used were sun-baked and flinty. There was no way out there. He ran his hand through his greasy hair. He was about to roar out, but he heard trudging footsteps. A silhouette passed the window, and he saw the guard with his rifle on his shoulder.

Cobb Orly raged to get out of there. He scurried to the opening, hissing, "Hey there, guard! Damn you, listen!"

The trooper halted and spun around.

"I can't stand it no more," Orly said. "I'm a'goin' to kill myself! I got me a knife! Had it hid in my boot!" He hurled the worn-out cot against the wall. There was the sound of brittle wood splitting.

"Hey, do nothin' of the kind!" the trooper hollered. In a minute, he'd found the sergeant, who joined him on the run. Keogh was a large and strong man, and he carried the key to the lockup in his hammy hand. He used the key and went inside, forgetting all about a lantern.

Orly came around in the dark with a clubbed bedpost and hammered the noncom's head. Keogh dropped like a pole-axed ox, and Orly leaped over him.

"Is that you, Sergeant?" The guard ran up, but he

saw just moving shadows. He hesitated to shoot. Orly clubbed him in the face.

Orly, as he ran, had never felt better. He'd seen his luck turn good. The guardhouse wasn't far from the corrals. He picked the first horse he could get close to, and thanked his stars again — it wore a hackamore. The bridlelike rig suited the deserter, considering the hurry he was in. He vaulted to the animal's bare back, wheeled and charged out through the gate he'd opened.

As he galloped past the hog ranch, he heard a flurry of shouts, but kept riding. He urged the horse to greater speed, and tore off in the direction of the creek. He splashed through the gravelly bottom and up the far bank, knowing that he'd just gained a fine head start. He couldn't be tracked before daylight, and by then he'd be well west on open plain.

Chapter Fourteen

"Nothing to be done then, Gilliam? Is Orly's trail lost for good?"

Phil Turnbo turned in the saddle so abruptly that his campaign hat scattered droplets. It was soaked, along with the rest of him. A brief but drenching rain had born down on the squad of troopers, leaving them as wet as rats drowning in a cistern.

The scout shook his head curtly. "His horse's tracks are washed out, Captain. Ain't no sure way of catchin' him now. Any way we ride, it's a long-shot gamble. Maybe we'll sight him, most likely we won't."

"Damn!" Turnbo knew that Major Cavanaugh badly wanted the deserter back. For every trooper in this man's army who lit out and got away with it, more were certain to follow. The dictum regularly proved true, even deep in Indian country. He slapped his McClellan's high, iron-hard cantle. "Damn!"

"It ain't like the feller's really free and sassy, Captain," Gilliam said. "It's a hell of a far piece up to Dodge or out to Santa Fe. And there's a hell of a lot of Comanches kickin' around 'twixt here and them towns. Totin' nothin' but hate for the White Eyes."

"Then your suggestion is that we turn back?"

Sabine Gilliam absently rubbed his bandaged left arm.

"Sergeant!" the captain shouted.

"Yes, sir?" Hoffman cried, riding up at the call. The noncom's long, flat face dripped rain.

"It'll be back to the post for us. There's no catching up with Orly now. Pass the word to the men, and take the opportunity to let them know that the redskins are likely to get him."

"I figure they know it already, Captain."

Turnbo nodded and waved, and the short column straggled in a turnabout. He didn't expect snappiness in such bad weather, but after a while, the sun broke through the gray skies and a rainbow bloomed. About midday, Gilliam pointed out the other cavalry column marching forlornly eastward on bone-weary mounts. Turnbo's men came up on D Company, with Lieutenant Ambrose at their head. The officers exchanged their usual friendly greetings. From then on, the last miles to the Cantonment on the Sweetwater seemed to pass more quickly.

"Didn't spot a single Comanche on the whole scout," the lieutenant complained bitterly. "And were we ready for them? Yes, we were ready, by God!"

Turnbo laughed. "That's why you didn't find them. Some of their hunting parties would've surely seen you."

"Leaping Wolf's a sly one, all right." Ambrose patted his gelding's side. "Declines to fight unless the advantage is all his way. Like any good commander, he hates to lose men."

"The Mexicans call it guerrilla fighting — it means fighting little wars."

A sarcastic frown crossed Nate Ambrose's brow. "Let someone who's died in one call it little!"

Sabine Gilliam felt at ease enough to speak. "But dead folks can't talk."

They had to ride past the great circle of positioned wagons, and even the most tired of the troopers stared curiously at the new arrivals.

"Emigrants, hey? When did they roll in, Phil?"

"Yesterday. That'll teach you to keep a company out scouting for three weeks."

"No time as yet for them to attract trouble?" Ambrose asked.

Turnbo shook his head. "This outfit shouldn't. No hell-raisers, only farmers, I'm told. Plenty of wives and young'uns under the bonnets of them wagons. Oh, and an unattached widow or two, maybe. Did I say no hell-raisers? I forgot one possibility. The wagonmaster himself's no New York society gentleman. Ever hear tell of a man called Sam Adler, Nate?"

Ambrose nodded. "I've heard a thing or two, 'cause I always keep my ears open. Adler's supposed to be a fine guide." As they passed the squat clutch of hog-ranch structures, Ambrose grew thoughtful. "Those so-called buffalo hunters been back? The one with the big nose and the other with the eye patch?"

"In for a day or two, then gone. Strange crew. Not likable."

Nate Ambrose's face looked somewhat happier. "Well, with Finn and Montooth not here, I confess that I'm relieved. I don't like fights breaking out in the saloon."

Phil Turnbo guessed the reason for Ambrose's remark. And then the troopers rode in files past the sentries and onto the cantonment parade.

After depositing his mount with an orderly and reporting to the commander, Nate Ambrose hurried to his quarters in officers' row. His nose told him just how badly he needed a wash. He stripped out of the uniform that he'd spent three weeks in and scrubbed, using a basin and Castile soap, his one luxury at the outpost. Rid of the worst odors of horse and sweat, he worked next with his razor. Less than an hour after riding in, he strode from officers' country refreshed, shaved and combed. The uniform he wore wasn't the least threadbare he owned, but it was clean. He headed for the hog ranch without more delay, despite the fact that the sun was still high.

Retta not only wasn't in the barroom, but she failed to answer when he rapped on the lean-to door. A turn about the outside of the establishment showed no sign of her. Off to one side of the saloon lay the wagon train's neat camp. Ambrose could glimpse people moving about inside the ring of wagons, but no fiery redhead caught his eye. In the other direction flowed Sweetwater Creek, renewed now by the rain and surging in its banks.

"Looking for something, Lieutenant?" The voice at his ear was husky, liquor-slurred, but definitely female. Ambrose turned to face a small, pale woman in a bright red dress. He recognized one of Jack Kyle's soiled doves and smiled pleasantly at her.

"Well, as a matter of fact, I'm looking for — "

"Retta?" The grin she managed was surprisingly pixyish for a whore past thirty-five. Her carmine-red lips twitched into a sly smile and she winked. "Look over by the stream, Lieutenant. I seen the card-playin' lady head that way a while ago. Figured she's got cause to do a bit of thinkin' by her lonesome. Don't all of us, bein' we can spare the time from our busy rounds?"

"Thanks, er — ?"

"The name I go by, is Cheri. Ain't that French and high-toned?"

Nate Ambrose came upon Retta Cantrell seated on a deadfall cottonwood. Sunshine filtered only intermittently through the pin oak, sumac and pale-leafed willow. It was the best excuse for a glade that part of Texas had to offer, cool by comparison to the unshaded prairie. She saw him coming and started to rise.

"Nate? Your patrol's come back? I-I didn't expect — "

He grinned. "Yes, I'm here and I'm real. It was rough out there this time because I can't get you off my mind. It's putting it mildly to say that I'm glad to see you, Retta."

She avoided his embrace by turning rapidly away. "Not now, Nate. Someone might see us."

"I can't believe you said that, Retta. You never cared about that before. I was always the one considering propriety, with troopers gawking about, or that damned Jack Kyle."

"Things are a bit different now."

"Different? How? The only thing different here is the new emigrant camp, and I hardly think that could be what you mean." His eyes narrowed as he studied her. "Unless that really does have something to do with this?"

Refusing to meet his gaze, she ran her fingers through her long, fiery hair, which was flecked with gold light. "I-I suppose there isn't any way out of telling you, Nate."

A rough, deep-pitched voice rang out. "Maybe I better tell the soldier boy, Retta!"

Nathan Ambrose never knew how the scowling stranger had gotten there. He simply appeared beside a clump of brush near the stream. Dressed in grimy trail clothes, with a holstered six-gun on his hip, he could have been a saddle tramp or a gunfighter, or worse.

"You ain't met me formal-like, Lieutenant, so let me take care of that. I'm Sam Adler. Now, about Retta, here, what I got to tell is for you to hear right good." He swaggered up close and started to talk. Ambrose had no choice but to listen.

The canyon was a great and impressive maw riven in the dun-hued flatland. Many hundreds of feet deep and just as wide, it plunged spectacularly in a riot of colored, sheer rock walls. The tiers of rose, brown and yellow limestone were tinged with vermilion and purple. The mouths of many lesser canyons opened in the cliffs, and miniature mesas reared like spires. In the depths of the colossal crevice flowed a river that never went dry. In some places, it spread broad and tranquil; in others it frothed between narrow banks of stone. Occasional pools of deep blue lay among the cedars, pin oaks and birch forest that dotted the bottom. A faint haze of mesquite smoke hung in a fragrant pall.

Cooking fires dotted the extensive tipi village where the canyon widened and curved. There were several scores of the dwellings made from buffalo hides stretched on cedar poles. The rancheria extended for nearly three-quarters of a mile. In the shadow of each fifteen-foot cone, naked children played — girls with dolls of plant husks and boys with tiny bows and arrows. Adults clothed in greasy buckskins either toiled or took their leisure.

Among the females, work was apportioned by status. Older or favored wives plied their hands at crafts such as stitching, beading and quilling, or cooked meals of fresh game and wild vegetables. Women who were less well regarded drudged at corn-hoeing, root-digging and hide-dressing.

Outside, Leaping Wolf's large tipi, Rushing Water Woman squatted, tending kettle and fire. The war leader's senior wife jabbered at her baby on its cradleboard, at the same time hacking prairie turnips for a venison stew. The infant stared blankly at the household's mangy dog. In the yard of a neighboring tipi, shriveled old men performed various tasks.

Near where the tipi flaps opened onto the littered yard, palid Moon Dove Woman sweated and struggled with a hide scraper. Made of brittle horn, the tool was difficult for unpracticed fingers to grip. The antelope hide, pegged to the ground, not only smelled bad, but was stiff, layered with decayed flesh and fat. The hair had to be scraped off, an arm-wrenching job. At Moon Dove Woman's elbow was a bowl of tanning fluid, a foul concoction of brains, liver and fat from the dead animal. The stench of it turned her stomach.

She paused to wipe sweat from her brow with her forearm, and toss a braid over her shoulder. The baby began to squall. Startled, the abducted white woman jumped, upsetting the noxious tanning fluid, and splashing some of it on decorative deer toes piled near at hand. Rushing Water Woman's chubby dark face swung toward her, scowling. A torrent of abuse in the Comanche tongue burst from her lips. And then the older squaw jumped up and came over.

A fist cuffed the smaller woman's ear, and she lost her balance. Gloriana Hollister tripped and rolled helplessly in the trampled grass. A kick caught her thigh, and another one her side. She gasped and squealed. The reaction only triggered more abuse. Rushing Water Woman dropped on her victim's chest with both knees. She felt rough hands yank up her skin dress, which was her only garment. Then sharp fingernails dug and scratched her. She was pinched on buttocks, abdomen and waist, while she writhed and recoiled. Then her breasts were attacked. Hot tears stung her eyes. She shrieked. From the sidelines, laughter erupted from gathered old men, women and some idle braves.

Then the largest, most powerfully built warrior in the encampment loped up. He raised his arms. "Ho!" shouted Leaping Wolf. The harsh lines of his fierce face signaled displeasure.

The furious squaw ceased the beating. There was conversation. Moon Dove understood only a little of it, since the gutteral words were spoken so quickly. Then most of the anger left the savage's features. Something must have been settled, because the war leader turned on his heel and stalked away.

Under the scornful eyes of the copper-skinned

gawkers the suffering woman cringed and rose slowly to her knees. Rushing Water Woman ran in close, her face hideously twisted. Her foot shot out, slamming Gloriana hard in her crotch. Layers of pain flooded her punished frame. She collapsed and passed out.

Chapter Fifteen

"Good idea, this, to have a party to honor the emigrants," Hazelcrest said to Marcus as they strolled through the late twilight after mess, their polished boots tramping the grassless walkway in front of the officers' quarters. They were heading toward the parade ground.

"It's to be a real party in all respects, Lieutenant," Marcus replied. "Of course, since we've no band and our only musicians are a couple of trumpeters, we'll wait and see what the music sounds like."

"I understand that among the emigrants are a fiddler and a banjo picker or two."

"I've heard that also." Marcus grinned, slapping the lieutenant on the back. "But will they be able to play dance tunes?"

The officers emerged from between buildings and into the open area. Lanterns stood on posts and swung from ropes strung from the flagstaff, a result of the troopers' labor. With the sinking of the sun, the full effect was impressive. The dance floor consisted of tarpaulins spread to keep dust from being raised by fancy-steppers.

A crude dais had been hammered together to accommodate the music makers in front of the quartermaster's storehouse. There was a refreshment bar to dispense a punch made from canned and dried fruit. All, to Marcus's eyes, seemed ready for a festive evening.

If it was a soldier's preference to patronize Jack Kyle's place, he was free to go there instead, of course. Marcus shook his head, amused. Likely the majority of the misfits would be hog-ranch bound in an hour, but the guests wouldn't even be aware of it. They would have their fun, enjoying the lights at night and the safety of the cantonment. The military garrison gave them more protection from Indians than they'd had for weeks. These days by the Sweetwater seemed like an island in time for them, at a place that could reasonably be called a true haven. No wonder the emigrants felt like celebrating.

Marcus and Hazelcrest circulated casually among the gathering crowd, which was about half emigrants and half troopers. The soldiers wore clean blouses, boots, kepis, even galluses, sponged and polished as if for a formal inspection. Little girls in frayed pinafores, little boys in patched britches — few with shoes — darted back and forth excitedly. There were unmarried youths and older girls, who were eager to pair off, hold hands and stroll. These seemed to congregate in the shadows at the edge of the lit area. And their elders appeared excited, too. Smiles were everywhere on the ordinarily gaunt, drawn faces of the sodbusters and their wives.

"It's a pity Turnbo's sentenced to the orderly room this night," Hazelcrest said. "But an officer of the day still has his duty."

"The luck of the draw," Marcus observed. "Where's Nate Ambrose, by the way?"

"Saw him washing and shaving earlier," said the older, swarthy officer. "But you're right, he's nowhere around here. Hog ranch, do you reckon?"

Major Cavanaugh shrugged. He'd just spotted something far more interesting than the officers under him. Virginia Keel had put in an appearance, strolling with Ezra and Charity Chandler over near the bandstand. Not even the musicians who had taken the stand distracted Marcus's gaze. And as far as their tuning up went, the tall major's ears had turned to tin. The widow was as slim and attractive as Marcus remembered. Her shoulder-length hair glinted with rich highlights in the lantern glow. Her facial bones were pretty, the mouth full of gentle humor. Her dress, with long sleeves and a modest neckline, became her well. At her throat, she wore an exquisitely wrought cameo brooch made of ivory — a touch that didn't seem out of place on the raw frontier. Virginia Keel, after all, was a woman with taste. Only her eyes hinted at sadness over her departed husband. Then she caught sight of Marcus, and smiled.

A fiddle, concertina and a severely cracked banjo began to play. The melody was a sweet old folk song in three-quarter time. The Reverend Chandler's sons swept their spouses onto the ground tarps to dance. Marcus made his way to Virginia Keel's side.

"Do you happen to dance, Mrs. Keel?"

"I always used to love to, Major. But now . . . "

There was a hesitation in the widow's manner that Marcus ignored.

"May I have the honor of this waltz, ma'am?"

"I, well . . . surely!"

At the officers' bar in Jack Kyle's hog ranch, Nathan Ambrose nursed a bottle of cheap brandy and sulked. Joe Finn and Bad Billy Montooth had been drinking for hours at a table in the back corner. The longer Nate Ambrose peered across the room at them, the more out of place they seemed. They were said to be buffalo hunters, but those of that profession usually spent long months on treks, wore clothing stained with blood and gore and showed up with wagonloads of hides enroute to railheads.

This pair spent a lot of time at the hog ranch near the cantonment. They'd arrive and depart with the same shabby teams and wagons. They'd talk for hours with the saloonkeeper, drink vile liquor and avail themselves of whores.

Nate Ambrose poured yet another splash of brandy into the tumbler he clutched. He tossed the disgusting drink off and winced at the assault on his stomach. The hour was still early. He wasn't drunk, but his upset condition had been building since reveille.

Yesterday, Sam Adler claimed Retta had once belonged to him and that he, the wagonmaster, reckoned she should remain so. Shocked and sickened, Ambrose had asked the redhead where she thought she stood. Retta'd hemmed and hawed, and refused to meet his eyes. Ambrose had stalked from the wooded stream bank angry and confused. He'd ordered his horse saddled and gone for a ride alone, braving the open prairie. He'd seen no Indians, but after a while he realized that Retta wasn't the woman he'd assumed she was. She held a strange attachment, one from a clouded past.

He resolved to be done with her. But that night, tossing on his hard bunk, the notion came to him that perhaps it wasn't her fault. Perhaps she did care for him but the claim of Sam Adler, frontier tough, held her an unwilling slave. Ambrose made up his mind then to see her again — tonight, when he was through with his army duties. Now he was in the hog-ranch barroom, but where was she?

Ambrose decided that he'd waited long enough and stood up, straightening his kepi. He strode past Finn, Montooth and Jack Kyle huddled deep in conversation, and nodded at several sergeants at the bat wings. In another minute, he was at the back of the soddy, trodding across the nearly pitch-black yard. He saw a bar of light under the loose-fitting slab door of the lean-to hut. He walked up and knocked insistently.

The voices inside stopped.

"Retta, open up in there!"

"Nate?" The officer's name was muffled through the panel.

"Yes, it's me! Who else? I waited in the barroom for hours, and you never came. Who's in there with you? Adler, I have no doubt!"

And indeed, the door was flung open by Sam Adler. The wagonmaster wore a sinister smirk, a tic twitching a muscle in his thrust-out jaw. His big right hand hovered near his low-slung gun. Ambrose's own sidearm — his .45 — was tightly buttoned under the flap of his cumbersome regulation holster.

"Well, good evenin' to you, Lieutenant," Adler said.

Ambrose crowded past him into the narrow room. Retta Cantrell sat on the bed, with her feet on the floor, fully clothed in a dress of calico. The front of the dress was rumpled. Her sea-green eyes were smudged and wide. "Are you all right?"

Retta nodded wordlessly.

"Adler, if you're here against the lady's wish, I ask you to leave."

"I ain't here against the gal's wish. I'm here 'cause I belong here. You might say to protect her from things that she might do."

"Let's permit her to speak for herself, Adler. Retta, I need to speak with you alone. If you don't want to right now, just tell me when — "

For the first time, Adler's face flushed with real anger. "No, you ain't about to palaver with her, soldier boy. She's lost interest in you. Now whyn't you clear out and let the gal be?"

Retta Cantrell burst from the bed. "No! There are some things I want to say to you, Nate. One is that — "

"Shut up, slut!" Adler stepped in front of the woman, thrust his arm out and halted her. She struggled briefly to get past. The Kansan brought up his hand and slapped her, the sharp blow brutally snapping her delicate head around.

"You swine," Nate Ambrose blurted, lurching forward. His fists were bunched and ready, but just then, Adler's right hand swept downward with lightning speed. It came up again holding a fully cocked Colt .44. The cavelike bore of the weapon was aimed at the officer's chest.

Retta, twisting away from Adler with surprising strength, pushed between the two men. "Wait, you two! Wait!" The harsh edge to her voice somehow reached them, and they froze. "Nate, you might take Sam's gun away, but there'd be a brawl, and if you killed him, you'd face court martial! Sam, if you shoot Nate, the whole army would be after you! There'd be nowhere you could run to and hide! Trying to kill each other for me — are you both fools?"

"You can't want what that man's doing to you, Retta," Ambrose hissed.

"I ain't lettin' the slut go!" Sam snapped. "She owes me too much!"

"Then there's got to be a fight!"

Retta Cantrell broke in. "You don't mean a duel, for God's sake? With pistols? Or sabers, maybe? Duels were outlawed years ago!"

Nate Ambrose backed away, suddenly more calm. "Then let's do it with our bare hands. Tomorrow, Adler? What do you say? Midmorning, after my company's done with drill? Over beyond the stream, where we'll be screened by trees?"

Sam Adler shrugged, making his compact but powerful shoulders bulge under his shirt. "Rough and tumble, soldier boy? With no holds barred? You sure you want to risk everything for the green-eyed bitch?"

"You bet your low life, wagonmaster!"

Cobb Orly felt like pure, unadulterated hell. He scanned beyond the plodding horse's ears and saw only bright, hazy plain. The same view met his eyes when he looked to his right and left. He twisted on the cavalry mount's bare back to glance behind for the hundredth time. He saw nothing but a sea of dry, brown grass and a few puff-ball clouds on the horizon. The sun's lemon disk was coasting up the sky. If hell really existed, then this was the devil's full-blown model of the damned place.

He'd ridden hard all night, and the animal was jaded. There had been no time when he made his break from the guardhouse to select a mount with bottom. He was in the middle of nowhere, riding a whacked-out horse. No saddle. No grub. No water. No gun. He'd seen plenty of game running about since sunup, but there was no way to bring a breakfast down. His strongest craving was for coffee. His throat felt like it was lined with grains of sand. And the sun's heat was like a branding iron pressed to his bare head. He longed for the hat he'd abandoned when he'd fled his cell.

For the third time in an hour, the horse stumbled. There'd been no water since Sweetwater Creek, which he'd splashed through on the fly. He'd pretty much stopped sweating, though his shirt was stiff with salt. For the first time in his life, he felt seriously scared. The horse stumbled again. It seemed lame, since it had been favoring the front off leg for miles. This time the animal stopped in its tracks and tilted like a listing boat. The rider threw his leg over and kicked himself clear. The bay flopped on its side and lay down, panting and heaving helplessly. And there'd be no way on God's earth to get it up again.

Orly studied the sky. The sun wasn't even at its glaring zenith, but its heat beat down like flames. Blinking through the haze, he fixed his eyes out across the flat expanse. He'd go on foot. He wasn't going to

130

let this damned country lick him.

An hour later, still trudging into the furnace wind, he tried to curse, but his voice was barely a croak. He was staggering himself now, far worse than the foundering horse had. A few steps later on the scorching ground and his knees gave out. His legs didn't answer his commands, and he sprawled backward.

His eyes were squeezed shut against the glare, but he forced them open. He was lying on his back, watching black specks circle in the sky above him. Damn buzzards! Then he saw something else that made the prospect of death from thirst seem easy. Feather-bonneted warriors were outlined against the sky. They were leaping from the backs of ponies, running toward him. Comanches! He watched helplessly, unable to move, as one brought a war club out and brandished it. But then, a tall, brawny redskin stood over the fallen deserter, glaring with hatred.

"Won't kill you here, Blue-coat," Leaping Wolf growled in the white man's tongue. "Too easy. Take you to our camp. Make sport for all my people. Ho!"

They dragged Orly up, tied him onto a pony and galloped west.

Chapter Sixteen

Nate Ambrose left the officer's quarters by the back route that circled the stables, and he was striding fast. He didn't need to consult his repeater watch to know he was running late. Sergeant Neal had buttonholed him after drill with word that Corporal Steinholtz's drinking was out of hand. It took several minutes to decide to strip the lax noncom of his stripes. Then the young officer hurried to his rendezvous with Sam Adler.

Lieutenant Ambrose didn't want to keep his rival waiting. All morning he'd been eager to smash the wagonmaster's face. Almost certainly, Adler would have beat him to the place set for the fight over Retta Cantrell. Ambrose rounded the corner of the low, farrier's shop and stood face to face with a grim Marcus Cavanaugh, who blocked the path. Ambrose threw a stiff salute and stopped for his commander.

"I'm glad I encountered you, Lieutenant," Marcus snapped. "If we hadn't happened to meet, I'd have sent the orderly to hunt you down."

"Major?"

"I want you to take Hazelcrest's place on patrol. F Company's answering to boots and saddles now. They'll be ready to ride within the hour. You'll be at their head, Ambrose, with Phelps as scout. You're to sweep south this time to take a good hard look for Leaping Wolf. If you pick up that missing deserter, well, all to the good, too, but I no longer have much hope there." Marcus launched into a few more details that Ambrose dared not interrupt. Finally he spoke up. "Major, I took out the last patrol."

"I mean to use Hazelcrest's knowledge of the country these next days while mapping my campaign. Not that I need an excuse to present you with! Pack your kit and get yourself ready to ride! You know orders when you hear them, Lieutenant!"

"Er, yes, sir. Thank you, sir!" Ambrose's face twisted angrily as he turned away.

"Oh, and Lieutenant!"

"Yes, Major?"

"You'll salute me when I've done talking with you!"

Nate Ambrose reddened, for there were troopers looking on. He gave a crisp, heel-clicking salute, which was returned.

Marcus watched the young officer hurry off, and stroked his mustache with a finger. Earlier that morning, just at reveille, he had heard someone banging on his quarters' front door. Retta Cantrell's appeal had been short and sweet, but urgent. She'd been correct in her fear that Ambrose's cavalry career would suffer severely if he took to brawling. This was true whether the promising young lieutenant won with his fists or not. Sam Adler would have to occupy himself by sitting on this thumbs for now, Marcus thought. The wagon train had to move out soon — and likely before F Company came back from patrol. The major strolled off leisurely toward the stables for a look at Champion. He felt good enough to whistle a cheerful tune.

Down the spectacularly vertical canyon face a trail descended, risky even for sturdy Indian ponies. The animal carrying the tightly trussed Cobb Orly wasn't the most sure-footed. Time and again the Comanche captive expected to slide off, beast and all, and meet his doom. Unfortunately, this was not to be. The steep downgrade reached bottom in a heap of crumbled shale. The hunting party bunched their mounts around his, their leader gave a hand signal and the group rode along the sandy level, noisy and exulting at what was to come.

They rode into the encampment at a trot, shouting and whooping enthusiastically. Squaws, old men and children ran out of the tipis and *jacales*. Some of the riders did horseback stunts, cavorting, rearing their ponies and exhibiting splendid horsemanship. They brandished feathered lances, coup sticks and clubs carved of buffalo bone. Sunbeams glinted on bright, new Winchesters.

Cobb Orly, who was weak from thirst, hunger and fear, could only tremble and whimper. Leaping Wolf tumbled the deserter from the pony's back and hooted when the captive flopped face down in the grass. Orly was only dimly aware of his surroundings in the chasm's depths, the towering cliffs, the trees, the dwellings. Shouts roared in his ears and his pulse raced. Or was the relentless thumping he heard the ominous thunder of drums?

Strong hands gripped the captive and flipped him over. A brief glance up at the cruel and gleeful faces drew a cry from Orly. "My God! My God! Say you ain't gonna work torture on me, are you? Don't! Kill me quick, I beg! Oh, Jesus, Jesus!" A vicious kick to his mouth quieted the wailing, and he was roughly hauled upright.

The males of the tribe seemed to have withdrawn from the center of the swale, leaving the prisoner, to his dismay, to the attentions of the squaws. They didn't get such fun often. Now they had a toy to tear apart. They knew it. Orly knew it. And the blood in the white man's veins turned to ice.

Leaping Wolf's face twisted, and his cruel mouth gave a shout to egg on the sport. At the signal, the women, ranging from young girls to aged grandmothers, closed in like fire ants to a feast. Clawing fingers ripped the outer clothes from the captive, and then proceeded to his ragged underwear and boots. In a minute, the white man was as naked as the moment he'd been born into the world.

Orly braced himself for the worst he could imagine. They began with kicks to his tender parts, and a hail of sticks and stones. The pale skin seldom exposed to sun was soon absorbing the cuts, scrapes and blows. Rawhide whips lashed him painfully. Blood beaded on the purple welts, then turned to rivulets. The captive was prodded, dragged and shoved, taking hits on all sides as he was herded along. They shoved him up against a tall pole that was branchless and stripped of bark and covered with innumerable brown-black stains.

Swiftly he was bound to the stake with stout thongs cut from deer gut. Pinned at his arms, ankles, waist and throat, he could hardly move. He felt the first knife cuts, which were shallow. Then the real destruction of human flesh commenced. The copper-skinned women leered. Orly knew his best hope was to show bravery, but he felt far from brave. Tears flowed down his face. Control of his bladder vanished, and he sprayed a stream of urine.

The women brought a devilish order to the ritual of inflicting agony. As if on cue, one of them at a time would scurry up to the bound, naked form to work some hurtful mischief, and then the next would take her turn. The first one sliced a shallow but bloody gash down Orly's chest with a fragment of sharp flint, and the next slammed his kneecap with a fist-sized stone. Another's contribution was a vicious tweak to his nipple with her fingers. A toothless crone used a pointed hide-scraper to punch Orly's abdomen. Each woman took her turn according to rank, the wives or mothers of the more renowned warriors going first and receiving more chances to probe or gouge. At each of Orly's cries, the inflicter of misery crowed with delight.

The most sadistic of the squaws was Running Water Woman. On her first pass at the white man, she applied a heated hatchet to his stubbled cheek. On her second, she scored the first coup on Orly's genitals, using a catclaw spine. At the victim's loudest yelp yet, the squaws tittered and danced with glee.

The warriors stood back and watched, voicing savage approval in occasional grunts, shouts or howls. Each minute was an eternity to the writhing, shrieking Orly. Soon the captive's skin from crown to foot-soles was reduced to shreds oozing bright crimson. Blood drooled from his ears and nostrils, where sharpened sticks had been thrust in and screwed.

By the end of the first hour, most of the females past the age of puberty had been given their chance at pleasure. But Moon Dove Woman, second wife of Leaping Wolf, had cowered at the sadistic Indians' roar. The former Gloriana Hollister was sickened by the gruesome spectacle. Knowing that she was expected to take part in it filled her with disgust and terror. She'd been taken in marriage by Leaping Wolf because of a whim. He held less regard for her than for a good pony. She was sure that if she made any more serious slips, he'd lose patience and kill her on the spot.

"Moon Dove Woman! Moon Dove Woman!" Gloriana heard her name above the tortured man's wails, voiced with familiar contempt by her nemesis, Rushing Water Woman. Leaping Wolf's vindictive older squaw elbowed through the throng, seeking her. The white woman tried to lose herself, but the rest of the women turned on her. She found herself thrust foremost among them. Directly across the trampled open space hung the bloodied form of Cobb Orly.

In her agitation, Gloriana scarcely understood the babbled words. Yet the Comanche gurgles and grunts assailed her, and the squaws' dark looks were stern. Rushing Water Woman thrust two stones into her hands. They were so heavy that her wrists sagged with the weight. She understood what she was supposed to do. She looked about her frantically, and her wild eyes met Leaping Wolf's. He stood well back from the women's antics, but what he wanted was clear enough. Cold fear racking her, Gloriana Hollister took one step, another, then rushed forward. In front of the bound, exposed man, she drew up, panting. Behind her, Rushing Water Woman fingered her rawhide whip. Leaping Wolf clutched his trade knife's haft.

Gloriana was terrified at the thought that she might die. She took mental aim, squeezed her eyes shut and hammered the rocks together, battering Orly's manhood. He vented a horrible scream. The squaws and warriors, roaring approval, advanced in a wild, mad rush. Knives and hatchets flashed and hacked, and in a few minutes, Orly became mincemeat.

There was a spark of life in the hideously maimed form, and it would remain for quite some time yet. But the center of action abruptly shifted at the rhythmic booming of drums. Fires were lit. Corn beer was brought out. Warriors produced war paint and smeared themselves. Some began to cavort and dance.

At the center of the frenzy, Leaping Wolf shouted boasts. He'd donned his trailing bonnet of eagle feathers. The scalps at his belt jigged as he shuffled to the beats. "Death to White Eyes!" he whooped, and whooped again.

A hundred warriors yelled, "Kill! Kill! Kill!" Painted faces grimaced, forms darted and retreated around the fires. It was the to be a long night of savagery.

The same moon that shone down on the canyon rancheria that night shone as well on the Cantonment on the Sweetwater. Across the open ground between the outpost and the encamped wagon train, Marcus walked slowly in the company of a woman. The tall major, in a relaxed mood, wore his kepi at somewhat less than formal tilt.

Virginia Keel looked especially nice in the silver moonbeams' pale glow. Her long legs moved gracefully, swaying her skirts along the tops of the crisp, dry grass. She used the handkerchief she'd taken from her cuff to wave bothersome insects away. Her smile wasn't forced, as it had been days ago, but brightly genuine. Still, she was more quiet than on the earlier strolls she'd had with the handsome major. Sam Adler had sent the word around among the emigrants that tomorrow at first light the wagons would roll to far-off Arizona.

"Pleasant night," she said.

"Pleasant, yes," was Marcus's response.

"Oh, Marcus, we just can't spend this last evening chatting about the weather."

He fumbled in his pocket for his stubby pipe of briar. "There's something that's come up between us, true," the officer said. "Oh, yes, I'm aware that exists, Virginia, all too well aware. It started the night of the dance — something in the fiddler's tunes made an officer on a frontier post start thinking this way."

"I know the feeling, Marcus. And in these last days I've seen the loneliness in you melt a bit." She smiled. "It gives a woman sort of a feeling of power."

As they wandered toward the stream, the eternal wind soughed and rattled the cottonwood branches. "So I have some admitting to do." The officer glanced at his pipe, and then across at Virginia Keel questioningly.

"Of course, you can feel free to smoke."

"All right, I believe I will." He struck a match, and the flame winked in his eyes. A few quick draws and the tobacco ignited. The smoke scent was rich and fragrant. "What I have to admit is that I'll miss you when you've gone, Virginia. Not only tomorrow, I'm afraid, but for a good deal longer. Now I'm an army man through and through, as you know. The military is my life and my duty for a good many years. Maybe duty will always be my first love. Just now I can't predict otherwise."

"I think I understand."

"Do you?"

"I've come into your life," Virginia said gently, "and we chanced to meet. Things like this happen. I'm in the midst of forgetting a great grief."

"Your husband's passing."

"And now I'm on my way to cross this great, wide land in search of a way to live out my days." She turned to face him. A smile played at her full, red lips. "I have some education, and these people I'm traveling with have many children. They'll need schooling when we reach the end of this trail. I feel I owe my services to the Chandler clan at least for a while. They've helped me so in my time of need."

"I see."

"So in the morning, I'll be sitting high in my wagon, Marcus Cavanaugh. Mr. Adler says our horses are rested again and fit. It should be a good, fast crossing of this Llano Estacado to the emigrants' promised land. And when we're settled on the other side, I mean to write to you."

The pipe had gone out. "If you do, you can be sure that I'll answer your letter."

140

"Shall we leave it at this, Marcus Cavanaugh?"

"I'd rather leave it at this." When he pressed his mouth to hers, her lips were tender and soft.

In the depths of the great canyon far to the west, the war leader Leaping Wolf raised an exultant whoop. He pumped his Winchester in the air and bobbed his magnificent feathered bonnet. All eyes in the encampment were upon him, except the dead eyes of Cobb Orly.

"War path!" the chief bellowed. "Kill all the White Eyes and Blue-coats!"

Roaring shouts erupted from the throats of a hundred braves. "Kill! Kill! Kill!"

Chapter Seventeen

The braided whips cracked, and teams of draft horses strained. The creaks of harnesses and greased axles mingled with the noise of scores of plodding hooves. The long line of Studebakers and Conestogas and Wright wagons snaked across the broad, unbroken plain. The sun blazed. Emigrants sweated and swore, but bore the heat.

Wagonmaster Sam Adler rode well out ahead of the train. The flashy claybank gelding that he straddled had a smooth gait, and he sat in his saddle easily. Straight-backed, alert and with his Spencer carbine resting across the bows, he swept the horizons with his cool, gray eyes. There was nothing to see but the endless grass plain and high sky. But responsibility for the safety of the wagon train belonged to the stocky, hard-faced man, and he maintained a careful watch.

Ezra Chandler yelled into the sifting cloud of dust raised by the teams. "Things look good, do they, Mr. Wagon Boss?" His wife, on the seat next to the reverend, squinted and smiled. Adler pumped his gloved hand and gave a lopsided grin, but didn't call back. In the following wagon, young and lanky Henry Chandler cracked his whip.

At least in this country, they didn't have to contend with grades, mountains or river crossings. Riding in the wagon beside horse-savvy Virginia Keel, Retta Cantrell gripped the seat with rigid fingers. The widow was a worthy reins-handler. For her own part, driving animals was a skill that she'd never quite taken to. Sam Adler couldn't have done better than park her with the Keel woman. Retta Cantrell slumped and heaved a sigh.

It was all for the best, she knew, her decision to accompany Sam when the train moved out. He was a brutal and thoughtless man, mostly, where women were concerned, but on the occasions when he was inclined to be even the least bit nice, his raw, sensual strength couldn't be denied.

She'd run away from Sam back in Fort Smith, vowing she'd never take a man again. Then she'd linked up with the decidedly questionable Jack Kyle in his hog-ranch venture. That there'd be no sharing of bedroom delights had been part of that deal from the first. The dark man had his soiled doves to vent his lust. She was a card dealer, a spinner of the betting wheels and a pretty face. Nothing more. But way out in Texas, with the cantonment across the stream, she'd grown starved for attention again. Along came Nate Ambrose, a few years younger than she was — and of course, he couldn't handle her, not really.

Now, biting dust under the hot sun on a jouncing wagon seat, she congratulated herself on making the right decision. She thanked God she'd averted the fight between Nate and Sam. She'd done right by Nate that one way at least. Nate could fight Comanches and gain recognition and promotion. What would he have gotten from battling tough Sam Adler? Even if he won, he'd set his cavalry career back forever.

"Thirsty?" Virginia Keel queried in a kindly voice. "Go ahead and tap the canteen under the seat. I'd like some of the wet stuff myself to slake one very dry throat."

"Good idea," the Cantrell woman said, reaching behind the seat. "Oh!" Her hand touched metal that had been heated by the sun. Fumbling behind her, she pulled a rifle onto her lap. "It looks like quite a fine one."

"The weapon my late husband used for years," said Virginia. "Sharps Creedmoor Sporting Model in the smaller .40-caliber type. It's light enough for me to shoot accurately. He taught me how to, by the way."

"What's this thingamajig?" She stroked the silver-chased breech of the weapon.

"Vernier rear sight for use at long range. And that other thing there's a spirit level. Luke could shoot the wings off a fly at a thousand yards. He hunted buffalo at one time."

Retta Cantrell frowned in interest. "I've never met any buffalo hunters myself. Some men who pretended to be, maybe." Her concentration seemed to lapse for a moment as she reached behind the seat again. "Well, now I have that canteen. Here, take your drink, Virginia."

"Thanks. Hungry, are you, Retta? We won't stop till we camp tonight. I've learned to chew dried beef to keep my strength up."

144

"Good idea."

"In the napkin-covered basket back under the bonnet."

"I have it . . . Oh, my God!"

Out in front on the claybank, Sam Adler sharply reined the animal about and waved his gun. A hoarse shout reached them, but the words were made unintelligible by the wind. Retta shaded her eyes and peered beyond the troubled wagon boss.

On a swell of ground against the horizon, an Indian warrior astride his pony was outlined against the sky, his feathered war bonnet bobbing and his scalp-decorated lance held high. As the emigrants aboard the wagons gazed, a long file of painted savages rode out of the concealed trough and fanned out beside their leader. Leaping Wolf kicked his mount's sides and gave a tremulous whoop. The pony burst into motion. As expert as any cavalry force in the world, the war party thundered across the plains, the braves firing repeating Winchesters as they came.

Immediately, the drivers of the lead wagons whipped their draft teams up to form a tight, defensive circle. Alone and away from the head of the train, Sam Adler leaned low to the claybank's neck and spurred for all he was worth. At least a hundred yards lay between the shrieking redskins and the wagonmaster, but the Indian's rifles were cracking.

Plumes of dirt spanged near the claybank's pounding hooves. Sam Adler turned in the saddle to toss return shots. The claybank's breathing made a harsh rattle, and froth strung from the bitted mouth. One of the warriors whipped his *grullo* pony to the front of the pursuing pack. Adler glimpsed the painted, howling face and the nine-foot lance the warrior

145

wielded by a braided wrist loop. The lance was tipped with a bayonet blade, spoils of an earlier raid. The fierce sun glinted on the angry point.

"Come on, horse! Run, Goddamn you! Run!" Sam urged under his breath.

Covering fire from the wagons broke out, but still the pursuers gained on the pursued, and the distance closed fast. Ahead of Sam, the wagon bonnets loomed and emigrants shouted. The urgent drumming of his horse pounded in Adler's ears. He turned and fired a shot behind him.

"Yaah-aaah-aaaah!"

The warrior was punched from the pony's back by the bullet, and he flopped in a cartwheel. At the same moment, Adler's horse was also hit. The claybank took a slug from long range, veered sideways and promptly dropped. Thrown, Adler rolled and bounded up, his legs pumping in a desperate, all-out run — ten yards, then five yards to the shielding wagons.

Retta Cantrell was standing among them, her hands clasped to her cheeks. Adler leaped over a fallen draft horse, dead in the traces, stumbled on a shattered whiffletree and plunged to the ground. He was helped to his feet by a couple of brawny Chandlers. One handed him a rifle to replace the one he'd lost.

"Thanks, fellers!" The wagon boss saw immediately that the emigrants had failed to form a defensive circle with the wagons. The Indians had shot quite a few horse teams quickly, and the wagons were strung out in a ragged line. It was Sam Adler's job to prevent a decisive attack that would overrun them.

"Men, and all you females, too! Get guns! Tumble trunks and such out on the ground! Hole up under the wagons! Shoot at every redskin that comes in range, and keep shooting!"

He watched the widow Keel take the Cantrell woman in tow, forcing her down behind an overturned wagon box, and thrusting a six-gun into her fist.

"Mr. Adler!"

The wagon boss spun to see Ezra Chandler waddle up. The reverend's face was stricken with shock and he spoke between sobs. "It's Charity, my Charity! Look, man! Look there!" What he pointed to was a mess. The stout woman had been hit by a large-caliber round. She slumped beside the corpse of a grandchild. Nearby a pet spaniel cringed, whining.

"Get yourself under cover, Chandler! This time it's kill or be killed!" He shoved the grieving man toward his wagon.

All around the improvised fortification, heavy rifle and six-gun fire roared. Acrid gun-smoke swirled in clouds. Wounded people screamed. Young Dolph Higgins was pinned beneath a fallen horse and couldn't pull free. As Adler looked on, the kid took a round, collapsed and was out of his pain. Off to his right, a pretty blond girl scampered, her arms filled with cartridge belts. An arrow pierced her back and she hinged over, dead before she hit the dirt.

The canvas tarp on the wagon next to Adler exploded in flames from fiery arrows. Emigrant defenders fled from the blaze's smoke and heat, but once exposed, they drew a different kind of fire, a rain of hot lead. An arrow-riddled man went down. His wife ran to him and met death head-on, her heart pierced by a flying bullet. This left the small family just one tiny infant, and it lay on the lowered tailgate, bawling. Another man tried to get to the child, but he was blown from his feet to die in turn.

On every side, Sam Adler saw disaster looming. One settler's head blew apart at the force of slug. A man with his shirt afire ran wildly until a lance cut him down. Hostile riders galloped among the wagons, howls and war whoops erupting everywhere. Smoke and fire raged through the wagon train.

Lem Carter shot from a crouch with his Greener scattergun, and a Comanche's pony spilled its guts in a gush. The warrior rider bounded back, swinging a hefty war club. Lem's brains were scattered across the face of the man next to him. Abe Chandler, the reverend's nephew, felt a lightning bolt of pain and looked down. A lance had speared his thigh. He blasted three hastily aimed shots at the redskin attacker, and saw a quill plate bloom crimson with blood. Abe fell, wrestled with the spear, then died when another brave rushed forward on foot and cut his throat.

The hideous painted face of the savage grimaced in glee. Sam Adler swung his Colt in that direction and blazed away. The Indian folded up and dropped. Adler emptied his pistol's cylinder, missing shot after shot. At last he hurled the useless weapon aside, drew his Bowie knife and ran at the tallest Comanche in sight. The man had painted his face, arms and chest, and had an arrogant, thrust-out jaw.

Leaping Wolf saw the wagonmaster coming and hurled his stout buffalo-bone club. The bulging knob joint struck Adler in the chest, and bitter nausea flooded the white man. He joined in hand-to-hand combat with the redskin, and found him greasy, hard to hold and extremely strong. The savage kicked his leg from under him. Adler clutched Leaping Wolf's long hair. Both men went down, grappling hard.

Sam Adler felt the bite of terror. He hadn't feared the weakling lieutenant back at the cantonment, but now he faced a real adversary. The Indian was an experienced fighter, but so was Samuel Adler. He slashed with the Bowie, but the enemy slithered aside. Leaping Wolf shoved an elbow into Adler's throat and slammed his groin with a knee.

Adler's knife spun from his hand, and Leaping Wolf scooped it up. Agony speared every muscle in the white man's frame, but he kept on wrestling. The knife point touched his throat, lingered a split second, then drove home. The stocky neck was sliced from ear to ear, the pale, pink tendons flipping free of skin and twitching. In the crimson gout of blood, Adler died, a shrill, cry of fury on his writhing lips.

Now it was Leaping Wolf's turn to scan the scene, and what he saw met his approval. On all sides the slaughter of the White Eyes went on ruthlessly. Only a few of the men and women remained alive still and unscalped. Especially interesting to him was the last stand being made by a pair of females. One was a brown-haired beauty and the other a flaming red-head. Virginia Keel and Retta Cantrell stood back to back, each with six-guns in both hands. They used them, too. Several wounded warriors squirmed at the women's feet. Others circled warily, declining to shoot.

Leaping Wolf approved. Raping the pair would be both pleasurable and cruel, but there was a way to inflict more pain and degradation still. He snatched up a bow and arrow from a dead brave, drew back the string and took aim. The first arrow took Virginia Keel squarely in the stomach. The second struck

Retta Cantrell under her right breast. Both women spun and dropped. But they weren't killed, as their agonized shrieks revealed. Not yet. Warriors swarmed over the downed women, tearing their clothing away.

"Now who will hold down the women?" Leaping Wolf demanded.

Volunteers jumped to do his bidding. Leaping Wolf and his brother, Lame Elk stripped down their leggings, and the women's baptism in the bowels of hell began in earnest.

Chapter Eighteen

"Jesus Christ and all His Saints!" the Irish guidon-bearer blurted out.

Trooper Nels Olafsen quietly retched into his campaign hat.

"Massacre! Worse even than the last 'un we found!" Said Sergeant Cal Neal who'd seen service at Cemetery Ridge, and yet his saddle-leather face turned the color of cold ashes.

Nathan Ambrose sat on his tall bay, rigid in every bone and sinew. The sight and stench assaulted him. Nausea flooded the young officer's guts. The company, which was drawn to this place of horror by circling buzzards, sat on their skittish mounts and gazed at the dead — horses, men, women, youngsters and babes.

The bodies of the emigrants had been horribly mutilated. Breasts had been hacked off women, and men's private parts reduced to crimson jam. Infant's heads had been bashed against wheel hubs or rocks.

Fingers had been cut from hands to be strung on medicine necklaces. All the victims had been scalped.

The lieutenant stepped from a daze, as did Neal and Long Jaw Phelps. "Move the horses around upwind, Sergeant, and tell them all to dismount," Ambrose directed. " A burial detail, if you please, to dig graves with field-kit shovels. But we'll walk through the wreckage and havoc first." He squinted at the scout. "Leaping Wolf's work, would you say?"

Long Jaw Phelps bobbed his long jaw. The gray whiskers bristled. "That's for sure, Lieutenant. Big war party. Took them settlers out right handy, yes indeed, and them armed as good as they was, too. Plus Sam Adler, none other, to lead 'em against the Injuns."

Ambrose, too, had spotted what appeared to be the corpse of Adler, though it was bloated and disfigured in a way that made recognition difficult. The coyotes and vultures had had all day to tear up the remains, and slimy entrails were strung along the ground like disgusting sausages. Abdomens had been ripped and organs devoured. And the carrion birds still jostled each other, competing for the grisly feast.

"Get rid of those Goddamned vultures!" Ambrose ordered.

"Yes, sir!" Neal exclaimed, waving some troopers forward on foot. "Practice with service revolvers, boys! Don't get much of it, ammunition costin' so dear, but now's our chance. Fire at will!"

The pop-popping of the pistols took over for a few minutes, and Ambrose welcomed the acrid smell of gunpowder over that of rotten flesh. Again and again the black birds' heads were blown from their feathered bodies. Wounded buzzards lurched and flapped with broken wings, looking even more grotesque than they did normally. Despite the rain of lead, the majority of the creatures ran clumsily and launched themselves into flight. Heavy from gorging, they winged off low across the empty plain.

"Cease firing!" the noncom barked.

"Now we go in for our closer look-see. What did the wise sage say? For this we are soldiers?" Ambrose inspected the mangled corpse of Adler only perfunctorily, noting as well among the dead the body of the train's organizer, Ezra Chandler. The officer wasn't acquainted with many members of the emigrant party, but he stalked about to gain facts for the report he'd need to make. The burned-out wagons framed a grim scene indeed.

On every side, there were more atrocities. Beheadings and dismemberments gave sickening variety to the mutilations done on this bloody ground. Some women had been selected for brutal rape, and others not. Ambrose saw no pattern to the selections. The ways of the savage couldn't be explained — that was Phelps's theory. Here it seemed to hold true enough.

"Lieutenant! Oh, Lieutenant! Over here, sir. Would you take a look?"

Ambrose swung about and followed the call of Private Verl Overton. The recruit was standing over a mangled female corpse. There was a lot of black dried blood where she'd been scalped, and more puddled between her bruised, spread legs. "This 'un I think the major needs to know 'bout, Lieutenant Ambrose, sir. I seen him strollin' with the lady on the post, like, well, er . . . like they-all was a-sparkin'?"

"Good God! Why, it's Virginia Keel!" After a brief glance, Ambrose could look no longer. He turned on his boot heel, only to be confronted by an even more shocking sight.

"Oh, God, no! Retta! You, too!" He staggered back from the mutilated, naked form. He hadn't known that the woman gambler had ridden with the wagon train, leaving him and his proposal of marriage to travel on the ill-fated journey in the company of the Sam Adler!

"Lieutenant Ambrose? Lieutenant Ambrose? Ain't you all right, sir?"

Tears of rage and helplessness welled in the officer's eyes. He steeled himself and gestured to the trooper. "Call the burial detail, Private. Let's get these unfortunates under the ground."

"Yes, sir!"

Turnbo walked into the commander's office at the cantonment, saluted and tossed his gauntlets casually on a chair. "Well, they're back again, Major."

"Finn and Montooth, who're supposed to be buffalo hunters? Over at the hog ranch?" Marcus, standing behind his desk, puffed the stubby pipe thoughtfully. "Damned suspicious. I said it before, and I say it again now."

"I know that's why you wanted a report when they next turned up."

Cavanaugh exhaled a cloud of smoke and frowned. "It's those rifles that are getting to Leaping Wolf. I'd hoped to plug the source before we made our big push against the Comanche, but already it's midsummer."

"The supply wagons are ready to roll, the men honed and the horses grained and strong. We've all the replacement troopers we're likely to get this year, and all the remounts, though we're still undermanned. Too bad we can't march with a full squadron, sir."

Major Cavanaugh shrugged. "With time running out, our schedule is to march when F Company returns." The pipe had gone out. Marcus stuffed it into his top drawer. "I've decided to do what we talked about before, Captain. It's highly illegal move we may have to answer for some day, but it could save time and soldiers' lives. And spell the difference between victory and frustration in our effort to pin down Leaping Wolf and force him to stand and fight." He glanced out the window. "It's nearly nightfall. I think Gilliam could have his best chance after dark sets in."

"I agree, Major."

"I'll wait in my quarters, expecting the report on anything of interest. We're desperate, in case you haven't realized."

"When you skew regulations, Major Cavanaugh, I know the stakes are very high. I'll tell Gilliam to be damned careful when he searches Finn's and Montooth's hide wagons. Even when they're drunk on hog-ranch crackskull, the two are gunslingers, and just as dangerous as Mojave sidewinders."

The trumpeter had blown taps hours before, but Marcus sat in the battered parlor chair in his quarters, staring at the wall. His eyes were directed toward President Grant's framed picture, but his thoughts revolved around Virginia Keel. He had no idea if she'd actually write him someday. In the meantime, he made no plans concerning her. His only concern had to do with the next campaign against the redskins.

It was hard for him to picture this land without an Indian threat and the army always two steps or more behind the savage enemy, a place where settlers could farm or ranch and raise families in peace. He regretted the shortage of troopers that had prevented an escort for the Chandler wagon train. With the sweep against the Comanches in the works, there wasn't a man to spare.

A light rap on the window made him get up and slide it open. Sabine Gilliam slipped over the sill and into the subdued lamplight. "Did you find anything?" the officer asked. "Anything at all to link the self-styled buffalo hunters with the Winchesters and the trafficking with the Indians?"

The swarthy scout took his time, but finally shook his head. He rubbed his hawk nose with a finger stained dark brown by tobacco. "If you want real proof, Major, you're goin' to have to whistle for it. No rifles in them wagons as of now, but then we never figured serious that there would be. Too risky to park close by the post loaded with gunnery goods. But there's somethin' mighty fishy, the way them wagon boxes are. They smell like hides, all right, but from years back. Most odd of all is that them wagons have got false bottoms. I used a knife blade for a pry and got a look. All empty, like I said."

"False bottoms?"

"Coulda held packin' cases like the Winchester factory uses. The right size, leastwise."

"Strange as hell, Gilliam. But hardly enough to question Finn and Montooth on. Damn!"

"Well, I'll be goin' then, Major. Get some shut-eye against a long day tomorrow. Oh, yeah. There was one other thing."

Marcus, too, had set his mind on rest, but he became alert at the half-breed scout's last words, and thrust his face close. "Yes? Go on?"

"Found this." Sabine Gilliam drew a buckskin pouch from his belt, loosed the drawstring and shook into his palm a cameo brooch nearly an inch in diameter. The carved ivory likeness of a woman's head gleamed. Recognition jolted Marcus Cavanaugh.

"I know that piece of jewelry. I saw it worn by a woman from the wagon train. I'm sure it's Mrs. Keel's brooch." He slapped the chair arm. "Why, those conniving thieves! How could one of them have — ?"

Sabine Gilliam raised an eyebrow. "Thieves, Major, got 'em plenty of ways to lift folks' things off 'em. Whyn't you just keep the pin, and give it back to the lady someday?"

Marcus grinned. "That's exactly what I mean to do."

"I figured you'd like to do it." Sabine Gilliam touched his old slouch hat's brim and left hurriedly. Fatigued, Marcus Cavanaugh went to bed.

The next morning, Lieutenant Ambrose arrived back at the cantonment and reported to the major.

"What in God's name are you saying to me?" Marcus Cavanaugh leaped from the cane chair behind his desk and stared at Ambrose. The young officer's uniform was caked with gray dust and yellow stains from horse sweat. His campaign hat brim sagged. His boots appeared ruined.

157

The young officer's mouth broke from its rigid line. "Why, I'm reporting what the company came on three days ago. The emigrant train that left here was hit by Comanches. The wagons are mostly burned. The people killed and butchered, every last one. A good many of the men and women we could identify. The Chandlers, Sam Adler, Retta Cantrell . . ." Ambrose hesitated and went on. "Virginia Keel was there, Major. I saw her body myself."

"Had she been — ?"

Ambrose gave a solemn nod. "Neither she nor the Cantrell woman had the chance to turn pistols on themselves. It went very bad for all the females, Major."

Even Phil Turnbo appeared affected by shock. Hazelcrest and Sergeant Keogh wore faces that could have been carved of granite. Marcus's expression was just as hard.

"What about effects?"

"The Comanches looted the train thoroughly. Took the usual things — guns, ammunition, food, coffee, liquor. And clothing, especially women's things. The squaws will end up with those in camp. They'll use the cloth, and any trinkets like jewelry will be — "

"Hold on!" The major's eyes squeezed shut. A vein in his neck pulsed. His teeth were clamped together, tight as a trap. "I've gone by the book at this post, just as always in the past. Citizens' rights respected. The line between the military and civilian law maintained. Now I think it's about time we forget proper procedure and try for results. Finn and Montooth might not have stolen that brooch before Mrs. Keel went with the wagons. It could've been turned over to them later, in partial payment of a debt for purchase of guns. A debt owed by Leaping Wolf!"

"What are you talking about, Marcus?" Turnbo asked. "Good God, man — "

"Get Sabine Gilliam in here, along with Phelps, Captain. And when that's done, I've got a mission for you and Sergeant Keogh. Yes, the both of you! Take a squad of six troopers, and make sure they're armed. Be ready to search the hog ranch and those so-called buffalo-hide wagons! Get it done as soon as you can. On the double! I want the answers to my questions by this afternoon!"

"Then?"

"Bring in Finn and Montooth. And while you're at it, that scalawag Jack Kyle! He's friendly with the two buffalo hunters and that's enough for me to tie him to them!"

"Yes, sir, Major! Right away!"

"One thing more, Captain Turnbo." Cavanaugh's voice rasped like a grizzly's growl. "I want those miserable excuses for men thrown in the guardhouse alive!"

Chapter Nineteen

They were both fairly large men, Finn and Montooth, broader and taller — in spite of slouching — than the soldiers of the cavalry who surrounded them. Outside the guardhouse, dawn tinged the pewter sky.

The cell was dim. The troopers had made good work of binding the prisoners back at their wagons where they'd been prodded awake by Springfield muzzles. There'd been half-drunk groaning at first, and when they saw the threat, a short-lived attempt to reach their gun belts. But Keogh's voice had taught the pair the error of their ways. "Move, boyos, and ye'll be cut down before ye can shake yer spalpeen legs!"

After that, it had been simple herding the two men into the guardhouse and shoving them up against a wall. Long Jaw Phelps and Major Cavanaugh strode in.

"Aha! So you came willingly. Too bad." If Marcus

Cavanaugh was abrupt, it was because he meant to be. He almost wished the troopers had been forced to shoot, official rights be damned. If the major's face was granite, it was only as hard as his resolve to get at the truth about Winchesters and rampaging Comanches. At whatever hardship to phony buffalo hunters. He sized up the pair, who stood in stinking buckskins, and their hard eyes glared back at him.

"We ain't done nothin', sojer," Bill Montooth grunted.

"Whatya bring us here for?" grumbled Joe Finn. His eye patch had been shoved a bit askew. "We be honest, upstandin' gents, by Gawd. You got nothin' agin us!"

"Keogh!"

"Yes, sir?"

"Break out the cords used to string prisoners up by their thumbs. We have us a couple of real hard types. The kind we always have fun breaking."

Phelps stepped forward with the requested objects.

"Jesus Christ," blurted Finn, "You ain't gonna . . . you can't. . . . Now, listen here, you sojer boys — "

"The hell we can't. Private McMurchison, Private Overton. Free up these hog-ranch studs' hands. Apply the braided loops. Aye, like that. Good strong-lookin' hands there, me buckos. Now a bit of dislocatin' — it'll work ill for yer six-gun draws — "

"We don't even know what we're s'posed to confess. So screw all you blue-coats, ever' last one! Includin' you, Mr. Ossifer!"

Marcus waited while Keogh lay the cords across the hands of Finn and Montooth. Then he fished out the ivory brooch. Thrusting the piece under the ugly noses of the two prisoners, he snapped, "Look here! This was found in your packs, men. We all know where this came from. It belonged to a lady in the emigrant train. At first I thought you'd stolen it from her wagon. But then we learned Comanches hit the train."

Marcus waited, studying the men. Their stubbled chins thrust out pugnaciously. Yet Marcus believed that he glimpsed fear in the man with the eye patch. So he bore down on Joe Finn.

"You!" Marcus grabbed buckskin and jerked the man. A trickle of sweat dribbled down the patch. "Talk, damn you, or we'll dislocate those thumbs you use to cock your buffalo rifles! Or do you drive those wagons out onto the Llano every few weeks with cases of new Winchesters under the boards? You'll rot in jail if you've sold guns to Leaping Wolf, Finn! But if you don't confess, you'll feel strong pain, starting now!"

"I don't know what you're talkin' about!"

Just then, Phil Turnbo burst through the door. "Well, we've got it, Major! The whole layout about the rifle sales. How this pair accepted gold and other loot from Leaping Wolf and gave the war leader new repeaters! That weakling Jack Kyle spilled it all rather than feel a branding-iron's kiss. No balls to the fellow at all," the captain said and smirked.

Gilliam strolled in with a poker glowing in his gloved hand.

The pinioned men grew several shades paler. "He told you, the polecat did?" Montooth was ready to chew nails and spit out the rust. "Lettin' on he was clean, hisself? Pshaw!" He spat. "Hell, he had a full share in it! If we go behind bars, so does he, by God!

162

The son of a bitch with his yellow backbone!"

Cavanaugh's eyes lit up. "You're going to tell us where to find Leaping Wolf, Finn." Marcus's voice was cold steel cutting ice. "So our troops can catch him unawares. Are you going to tell us now or later?" The major looked over at Gilliam's hot poker.

"Say nothin', Joe!" Montooth advised. While he was rattling his tongue, Long Jaw Phelps peeled open Finn's shirt. The one-eyed man trembled with fear. Gilliam spat on the iron's hot end. The saliva hissed and crackled.

"So, do I go ahead, Major?"

Marcus's eyes were squeezed shut. Behind the tightened lids, he saw faces: Retta Cantrell's and Sam Adler's. These were joined by the vision of the Chandler clan: Ezra, Charity, the sons and their wives and grandchildren. He thought of shavetail Hayes Bingham. But the foremost face in his mind's eye was beautiful Virginia Keel, who wore a bittersweet smile. "Yes, if he won't talk, burn him," Cavanaugh ordered.

Sabine Gilliam moved his arm slowly, bringing the poker close to Joe Finn's chest. Sweat poured down the one-eyed man's face. Just as the heat of the iron caused his skin to redden, Finn broke. "All right! All right! Put that damned thing up! Leaping Wolf's rancheria, where the whole band stays, squaws and all, it's down in a deep canyon that's in the Llano. Ya don't believe such a thing's there, but it sure's Hell is. If you want, we'll ride three days south and I'll show you! We're expected in a few days, fetchin' the biggest gun shipment yet. Maybe the redskins can be jumped in their tipis! Wouldn't that be fine? But you'll need a lot of troopers, Major! The red niggers

163

got better guns than sojers! And not a single bad shot among 'em!"

"Hear that, Phil?" Marcus asked Turnbo.

"We all heard it." The captain was grinning from ear to ear. "And it sounds like all we need. By the way, I lied for the cause. Kyle let out no secrets at all. He was so scared, he collapsed."

Marcus spoke rapidly. "Get the word to the men. Boots and saddles directly after morning mess. All the companies will be going on this one, except a skeleton force to defend the post. I'll take command of the march myself. There'll be a conference of all officers, in the orderly room one hour from now. If anyone's late, God help him!"

"Looks like we'll take 'em this time, Major!"

"We'll send them down to hell to meet the devil, Captain Turnbo! Or we'll damned well all die trying!"

As the morning sun edged into a sky of indigo, C Company filed across the Sweetwater Creek. The other units followed in good order, troopers and officers tall in their saddles. The horses, fresh and nourished with grain, stepped out eagerly. The noises of creaking leather and jingling bit chains made soft litany. Sun glinted from metal.

The blue columns swung south, double-ranked, pack mules in the rear carrying water kegs, spare ammunition and food. They were crossing dry country in its driest season, and the commander had no intention to turn back before engaging the Comanche.

Marcus rode the leggy black Champion ahead of

the guidon-bearer, Turnbo sitting saddle to his left, Gilliam to his right. Once they'd left the environs of the outpost, the scouts would range ahead for miles if need be. But for now, no one expected fresh Indian signs. The squadron knew its destination from the words of Finn and Montooth.

Marcus had decided that bringing the bogus buffalo hunters on the mission would be a waste. There were fleas and bedbugs in the guardhouse that would appreciate something to bite. That's where, together with Jack Kyle, the confessed gun traders languished. The three of them could swap lies on gun-running profits before they were hanged.

Marcus turned in the saddle and scanned back down the lines. Through the dust pall, he made out Keogh and Ambrose with their troopers. Hazelcrest had stayed to command the outpost. "A fine day for it, gentlemen," the major observed. He was as eager as the horses, but his face was grim. He still pictured Virginia Keel, dead at Comanche hands. He tried to forget, but failed.

"Yes, fine day, sir," Phil Turnbo responded.

"The way the old Indian expression goes," Gilliam said, "it's a good day to die."

"Then let the red hellions die," Marcus offered harshly. "This war has gone on too long. Now we can take gun and saber to the enemy and finish them off. Your understanding, Gilliam, is that in this big canyon there'll be ways to pin down the band, block escape and bring off a battle that's decisive for once?"

"Me and Phelps and the Tonkawa scout, Menewa, will be goin' in ahead. We'll find a way it can be done, I reckon."

A towering dust devil — a great, swirling mass of

circling air — passed slowly in front of the companies, sweeping dust and debris aloft to form a dark column against the sky. The slowness with which the gust moved had an eerie quality.

"Ho, a sign," Sabine Gilliam said. "Or so my mother's people, the Delawares, would say. But something like this, it don't mean good luck always, Major Cavanaugh."

"What then?"

"If you care to know it, there'll be bloodshed ahead, much bloodshed. On both sides of the battle that's to come. Not just the enemy's side."

"I never figured this for a Sunday-school picnic, did you, sir?" Turnbo said.

"Not at all, Captain. Not for a single minute."

By the third day, dust covered the men and horses in dense white layers, lending a ghostly appearance to the marching force. By now, they were weary, fed up with long hours of riding and scanty meals of hardtack and salted beef. The men slouched in their saddles under the weight of the Springfields slung over their shoulders, but they grumbled little, considering. This deep in untracked Comanche country, there was something more important than complaints. It was wariness.

Gilliam and Menewa ranged far ahead and returned with news. The column was approaching the great canyon that Finn and Montooth had described. It was deep and broad and colorful, a fine place to hunt, fish and camp. But that wasn't what the cavalry from the cantonment planned to do. They had ridden out to make war.

The imposing rim was reached at midday, and the scouts showed the commander the trail downward. The yellow limestone was broken and crumbled. At first glance, it seemed impassable for goats, much less cavalry companies.

Marcus swung down from Champion and passed the order permitting troopers to rest and smoke. He moved to the edge of the low shoulder that shielded the drop-off, crouched beside Sabine and uncased his field glasses. Far in the depths, he saw water, green grass and trees. He knew the trees were of good size, although from the rim of the canyon they looked like shrubs. The major took many minutes to scan the terrain below. There was no sign of movement in the chasm. "The Indians haven't posted sentries? Or is it that they're well hidden?"

The scout pursed his lips. "I've seen no lookouts, Major, and I tried my best to find some. Neither have Phelps or Menewa found any. I reckon Leaping Wolf's sure he's safe down there. He thinks the blue-coats don't know about his camp. Indians are more like white folks than you suppose. Nobody among 'em wants to pull dull sentry duty whilst there's game to hunt, loafin' and gamblin' to play at."

Marcus nodded. He was still using the glasses, studying the apparently lifeless slopes below. Shrubbery lined the trail down the immense cleft's wall, and the loose shale and rotten rock looked dangerous. Disastrous slides were possible any time, and risks would increase with disturbance by foot or hoof. A successful descent would require care and luck.

"This is the only way down?" Marcus demanded.

"We looked for miles, Major. Saw nothin' else."

"Then we'll take it."

"It's what I figured you'd say, Major. Want me to pass the word you want to talk with the sergeant?"

"Do that."

Ten minutes later, the leaders led the men over the rim. It was with such a narrow trail of curves and sharp switchbacks that no cavalryman's horse could be turned around. Stirrups scraped the cliff face on one side, empty air on the other. Looking outward, the men peered down on eagles and hawks soaring high above the canyon floor.

"Jesus Christ," exclaimed Captain Turnbo as his bay stumbled at the lip of the precipice.

"Mother Mary," Sergeant Keogh muttered, his own mount missing its footing, but then saving itself.

Lieutenant Ambrose had the closest call of all. A shelf of rock gave way, forcing his horse to leap in panic. Hooves dug and haunches strained, but the animal managed at the last possible instant to scramble to safety. Ambrose vented no curse, oath or prayer. He only scowled over the image of Retta Cantrell that he couldn't forget, bloody and hideous in her last death agonies. And he thought silently of what he aimed to do to Comanches with his own guns and the guns of those he led. If the devils had wrought slaughter on the white settlers, he'd wreak double measures of fury on every warrior he laid gunsights on.

At the front of the sweating, fretting column, Phelps was talking to Marcus over his shoulder as he rode. The hooves of the horses clattered on stones underfoot. "Careful, now, Major," the scout was saying, "there can be rattlers on these here ledges. Like to coil in the shade they do, and can strike a feller afore — "

A shot rang out, its report echoing up the chasm's walls. Phelps clutched his chest where bright crimson stained his buckskins. He grunted. The scout tilted in the saddle, which unbalanced the horse and made it misstep. Man and mount toppled from the trail and went pinwheeling into space.

Chapter Twenty

Marcus saw smoke bloom from a shelf below, where piled rocks concealed the enemy marksman. He reined his mount up with a gauntleted hand and signaled those behind him to halt. "Weapons out! But for God's sake, men, don't try and dismount. Lay down slow and steady fire in the direction of the ambusher as we advance. There's no way out of this but down the trail. All right, let's go forward!"

If they had to ride into the maw of hell, they would do so, but that might not be necessary. There'd been only one shot fired, which suggested one Indian ambusher — possibly a hunter or a posted lookout.

Marcus felt an icy sensation on his chest under his sweaty blouse, as if somewhere, some unknown man was taking aim at him, the blue-coats' leader. Still, he guided the black horse with a steady hand. Behind him, regular as the pulse of his repeater watch, shots were being fired by the troopers. He saw another smoke puff farther down the slope, and from the file behind him, he heard a cry of pain. A soldier had been hit. The troopers' gunfire redoubled. He saw a redskin wearing a single eagle feather flop into the open below, clutch his chest and fall across an outcrop. The men congratulated one another, quietly, perhaps, but towering in enthusiasm.

"Atta way, Devlin!"

"Chalk up another for ol' Harley, my man!"

"And don't ya forget thanks to his Betsy gun. Lord, but he can handle that piece at long range!"

Marcus smiled. The outfit's top sharpshooter had scored importantly this time, killing the Indian and permitting them to ride on downward. But the major well knew that the gunfire must have alerted other Comanches. It was only a matter of time before his troops met stiff resistance. It was vital to get down the treacherous trail without delay. He welcomed the sight of the bottom of the canyon when he saw it. The brutally steep incline lessened. The last stretch was a great talus of rubble.

At last, the men found themselves on level ground. Before them, the troopers saw the mirror-smooth river, which was broad and shallow. The major waited for Gilliam to come up and give his opinion. Nothing would be worse now than miring horses in quicksand, turning the command into sitting ducks to be cut down by Leaping Wolf's braves.

"It's safe to cross," the scout reported. "I can see the play of current around the rocks and between the banks. No eddies, no bars. The bed'll be gravel, and for sure not foot-grabber sand."

Marcus nodded.

"We'd best cross as soon as possible, Major." The breed scout pointed upstream. "Smoke from up top tells me the big camp's up that way. Them shots'll bring Comanches quicker than spit, I'm bettin'. Good to be where we can take cover when they strike."

"It'll be done." Marcus turned and shouted. "Keogh!"

"Yes, sir," the top-kick roared, riding up the line of troops.

"The crossing won't be bad, Gilliam says. But let's lose no time. First troopers across will form a skirmish line, mounted, of course. Stand ready to protect the others. We could start to see resistance soon. Leaping Wolf knows we're down here by now."

"Aye, and I'll pass the word, sir."

It didn't take long. The troopers splashed through and regrouped beyond the stream. Gilliam and Menewa ghosted off toward the upper reaches of the canyon to warn the men of approaching hostiles and, if possible, spot the encampment. Without the advantage of surprise, the cavalry's task was risky.

Marcus told his plans to Turnbo and Ambrose while the columns were reforming at the sergeant's direction. "There'll be an advance party that I'll lead myself, flankers off to left and right. The companies following will carry rifles at the ready and be prepared for attack at any time. If we're jumped by hostiles and it's necessary to dismount, horse holders will lead the mounts to the nearest cover. It's a damned shame when cavalry must fight afoot. We lose the advantage of swift-striking power and our ability to cover ground. But it's tight down here." He gestured up at the ribbon of sky beyond the rimrock. "If it's what's needed to flush the Comanche, it's what we'll do."

Phil Turnbo had a question. "You're not expecting

the enemy to try and slip away this time, Major?"

"No. I expect him to stand and do battle. Even bring the fight to us."

"It's what we've wanted all along," Nate Ambrose said bitterly. "This is our first real chance at them."

"We'll hit them with all we've got. And outnumbered or not, well, a United States soldier is worth at least ten savages."

Smoke from the many cooking fires drifted lazily in the soft breeze. The women worked at tanning and other chores, while the children played games. All seemed peaceful. Then the first distant shot rang out, followed by others in a pattern that signaled danger. In front of his tipi, Leaping Wolf jumped to collect his weapons. These were never far from his hand, even here in the hidden sanctuary of the great *barranca*. In addition to the two knives, the war leader carried his flint-studded war club of bone and his Winchester.

As he checked the loads, warriors ran to him shouting, "*Hsosis! Hsosis!*. Have the White Eye devils come?"

"If they have, we will drive them back, killing many," Leaping Wolf cried, running for his favorite pony. "Follow me, my brothers! We ride to where the trail comes down the great cliff. We will take to hiding places, shoot our enemies and gain many scalps!"

Pausing for the armed warriors to group, the war leader's gaze fell on Moon Dove Woman, huddled in the tipi's shadow. She looked even paler than usual, ill, perhaps. If she sickened and died, it would be no great loss to the band. Leaping Wolf turned away. As soon as most of his able-bodied men had massed, he let out an ululating cry. The warriors on their ponies galloped up the draw, as mangy camp curs scattered from their path.

Rescue? The word crossed Moon Dove Woman's mind hesitantly. She'd been held captive so long, she dared not hope. Running Water Woman and old Squatting Badger rushed up, jabbering about hiding in the brush if the enemies forced the warriors back. The encampment's last line of defense consisted of untried youths and "brow-strap" males — those who preferred each other to mating with women, and whose fighting was traditionally confined to rear-guard action.

But the soldiers probably wouldn't withstand the Comanche thrust. Leaping Wolf was fighting in his own territory on his own terms. His strong medicine spelled invincibility.

Gloriana Hollister started to sob. Soon, though, she was swept up in the bustle of the squaws' preparations, forced to take part or take punishment.

The troopers rode between granite monoliths where the canyon narrowed. Marcus led on big black Champion, more watchful than ever, casting his eyes ahead, to the sides and up the rock walls, which were studded with outcrops. There'd been no sign of Gilliam or Menewa for many minutes, and he knew all too well that the scouts might never be able to rejoin the column.

When the canyon funneled between miniature twin buttes, he called a halt. At the horses' feet, the river frothed and tossed, attempting to burst its banks and race to lower levels. Thrusting up from the soil were perpendicular columns of eroded basalt, split with crevices, which made fine embrasures for concealed riflemen.

Beyond the gap, there was no telling how the land might lie. Without information from his scouts, Marcus Cavanaugh weighed pros and cons for several seconds. Time was running out. He made his decision and waved Keogh, Ambrose and Turnbo to his side.

"If there's a chance at outsmarting Leaping Wolf," Marcus told the others, "this looks like the place to make our try. It's only natural for him and his warriors to bring battle away from the camp, so I'm counting on their being enroute down canyon. In fact, we're lucky to have got this far. Captain, I want your troopers up in those clefts with rifles. Send your mounts — all of them — to the rear with a few horse holders. That will leave Ambrose's and my detachments to proceed slowly up to that gap we see — the one that the Comanches will come through."

The major grinned wolfishly. "When the trumpeter blows retreat, the mounted companies are going to fall back into range of the clefts. You should have the firepower to obliterate a brigade. Use it on the warriors. Oh, they'll try and escape back up the canyon, and might succeed, but only with a crippled force. Our main party, regrouped, should be able to press on their heels and clear the way to the camp. Questions?"

"None, sir," Ambrose said curtly.

"Seems pretty clear-cut. But about the scouts?" Keogh asked.

"They should be able to guess what we're up to

when the shooting starts. Once we fight our way through that notch, I expect to see them again, with all the advice we need to cut the hostiles' horse herd and pin them in the village."

The preparations went with smooth efficiency. Soon the C Company troopers were scrambling up the slopes. The ankle-deep loose shale didn't make for easy going in the stifling heat. The snipers were no sooner in position than Comanche warriors broached the great pillars on either side of the trail. Some had taken a few minutes to don war paint. All were armed to the teeth. They pressed their sweated ponies in swift lopes. When the Indians saw the mounted cavalry, chilling, high-pitched whoops rang out.

Score upon score of Comanche hostiles, a seemingly endless chain, pounded across the flat banks beside the river. Leaping Wolf waved his Winchester and kicked the pace up, his heels drumming the racing pony's sides. Soon the whole horde moved at a roaring gallop. Guns started to pop at extreme range, but Marcus's order was to hold return fire to save cartridges. The troopers on horseback reined in and held their ground, waiting for the savages.

If the enemy got too close, Marcus knew, it would be hand-to-hand combat with guns and clubs. It was the Indians' habit to turn mass conflicts into individual acts of bravery. The cavalry didn't plan on waiting for that to happen. A scattered volley launched by the savages kicked up divots in front of the soldiers. Finally, Keogh relayed his major's signal.

"All right, me boyos," the big Irishman bellowed. "Give 'em a bitter taste of it! Fire at will!"

The formidable booms of Springfield rifles suddenly overpowered the racket of hoofbeats and Winchester reports. Indians toppled from their mounts, but the charge roared on. A trooper on a wounded bay was pitched from the saddle. He landed upright and running, but was blown from his feet by a winging slug. Private McMurchison fired a round past his mount's ear, popped the trapdoor on his breech and rammed home a fresh round. But before he could fire, he took a slug in his face. Brains splashed out the back of his shattered skull.

Nate Ambrose fingered his Colt revolver and waited. Leaping Wolf bore down on his company's right flank. Under the steaming onslaught of bullets and arrows, the soldiers' line suddenly fell back toward the center. Ambrose was left out in front, exposed.

"For God's sake, sir," Sergeant Neal shouted. "Fall back! Fall back!"

Instead, the lieutenant spurred out, challenging the war leader. Leaping Wolf's calico veered. The warrior scooped a wounded brave from the ground and swung him up behind. As the double-mounted riders sped back, there was no chance for a clear shot.

Ambrose joined Neal, and they fell in among the troopers who were milling their mounts. As the redskins regrouped and renewed their charge, the whole blue line answered with ragged fire. The line dropped away. The warriors raced back and forth in a no-man's land of sprawled corpses, giving vent to ferocious war cries, darting at troopers to loose an arrow or hurl a lance.

Then the flurry of gunshots from the troopers ceased. The trumpeter signaled a retreat. The clear, brassy notes bounced off the canyon walls. The men of the companies turned their horses and dashed downstream. Iron horseshoes sparked on stones, and filtered sunlight glinted on their metal accoutrements. As the fragile line wavered and broke, the Comanches raised their loudest cries yet. Leaping Wolf and his followers kicked their ponies into headlong runs. They chased after the troopers with the fury of whirlwinds.

When the trumpeter stopped blowing, and a volley of shots from the soldiers concealed in the face of the cliff thundered out. The roar was deafening. Bullets poured like winter sleet, ripping into the backs, heads and chests of surprised Comanches. As the fissured canyon walls spat death, the main body of Comanche braves scattered. Some tried to return shots. Most of them jerked their mounts' heads violently around with jaw ropes, kicked and fled up the canyon toward the gap.

The buckskin stallion was shot in its lung and went down, crushing the screaming rider. Another brave's lance lowered and lodged in the dirt. His horse continued at breakneck speed, flipping the rider and breaking his neck. One Comanche's war bonnet was torn from his head. The young warrior turned on his mount's back and shrilled defiance. A 240-grain slug erased his painted nose, and his pony crashed into another Indian's. Both braves pitched to earth, and their faces were sliced to bits by running hooves.

Marcus Cavanaugh, riding at a gallop, exulted at the sight. The momentum of the cavalry was rolling. The horses' shod hooves rang on rock as the troopers gave fast chase. From positions on the cliffs, Turnbo's company still laid down dense fire. The panicked warriors swarmed between the looming boulders. Cavanaugh's cavalry thundered after them, sensing victory and lusting for it.

Chapter Twenty-
One

The troopers raced across meadows, tearing through stands of dwarf cottonwoods and spruce. They drove the fleeing warriors of Leaping Wolf's band ahead of them, up the winding canyon. The redskins' stand would be at the rancheria itself.

Marcus Cavanaugh spurred Champion along in the front rank of his men. If he knew anything about the Comanche war leader, it was that he was full of tricks. The cavalry had just pulled off a trap of sorts, using riflemen positioned on the canyon walls. Now they had to beware of having the tables turned. The best bet was to press their advantage while they could, hound the savages to ground and round them up.

The troopers fanned out and fired, sweeping around another bend with the sound of the charge bugled in their ears. Marcus glimpsed a pair of familiar horsemen cutting toward him from a side slope. Gilliam and Menewa guided their horses through stipplings of mesquite and catclaw. The breed scout rode like a demon, his long brown face awash with dirt and sweat.

Beside a colossal sandstone slab, the major reined up in a cloud of dust to await the oncoming riders. In less than a minute, they slid to a stop beside him. "Gilliam! Menewa! What news?"

"We've had us a look-see at the camp, Major, and it's a big 'un!" Gilliam explained. "A clean ride 'twixt here and there, so let the troopers keep on goin'." The piebald gelding the scout straddled tossed its head in lathered excitement. "But once those men hit the tipis, count on hell. Boulders everyplace! Deadfalls, trees and brush! Didn't see no way out for 'em on t'other side! Leaping Wolf's bound to make a stand, and a hard-fought one."

"So it won't be an easy ride through?"

"Another massacre like Washita, soldiers killin' squaws and kids? Hell no, sir!"

"Glad to find out the situation. Now let's catch the others. I'm hearing gunfire again!" Marcus gave spur and wheeled the black. The animal gave a leap and charged up the canyon with the two scouts right behind him.

Soon enough, they were in the midst of it. On all sides, hooves pounded the sandy soil, the solid mass of cavalrymen sweeping the edge of the encampment and darting among tipis. The chatter of carbine fire drowned out the trumpeting, and bullets whizzed like angry bees, riddling the hide lodges. From the tipis, Indians burst forth, not warriors, but the elderly and young. An outraged squaw ran in front of a

180

trooper's horse and flung a kettle. The trooper shot her through the forehead and galloped onward.

Old Sleeping Turtle tottered forward, toting an ancient Hawken muzzle-loader. He tripped on a root and fell headlong in a horse's path. The battering hooves crushed him. Trooper Cy Carter shot the next Indian he saw with his heated six-gun. It was a twelve-year-old clutching a two-foot bow. The small corpse pitched into a cookfire, its clothes sprouting flames and smoke.

There were casualties on the blue-coat side as well. Corporal Hennessy's gut was punched by a bullet from Eagle Claw. The noncom splashed into the river and didn't come up. The remount horse plunged away, kicking and sunfishing until a warrior grabbed its bridle and swung aboard. Riding into the fray and swinging his war club, the Comanche killed the guidon-bearer.

Warriors fired from behind trees and boulders around the camp, while others raced on horseback plying rifles and lances. One of the bayonet-tipped spears plunged through Private Gib Franklin's lungs, and the trooper vomited blood until he died. Meanwhile, Leaping Wolf's brother, Crazy Fox, lost his pony to withering fire. The warrior's neck snapped when he hit the ground, and the pony herd that he was guarding burst the rope corral. The animals bolted across the tumultuous battleground, trampling women and children, and causing cavalry mounts to shy and spoil their riders' aim.

Up and down the lines, the cavalrymen made their shots count, ignoring the bullets that sang back to them as they dealt death. Here and there, troopers struck by arrows crashed to earth, screaming. Others, on the ground but unhurt, took on crazed warriors hand to hand. Pistol butts met battle hatchets, and men holding rocks encountered sharp knives.

Private Niles Pruitt slammed a stone to the temple of Bear Claw, sending the Comanche reeling. But the trooper was jumped by Crow Wing, a brawny, broad-faced brave with a trade knife that he wielded fiercely. With a wild upward slash, the pony soldier's intestines spewed out. As he spun away, howling, another brave ran to praise his brother. But congratulations were cut short when hot lead scythed both Comanches down.

Sergeant Keogh shot a warrior, freezing the amazement on his ugly copper face. Across the camp, Corporal Deal Otis shot the Comanche named Three Trees. He laughed raucously, then pivoted to see a mounted warrior bearing down on him. He threw his rifle to his shoulder to shoot, but misfired, and he was forced to use the weapon as a club. Thunder Hawk's lance dipped and impaled the trooper's thigh. Otis's gun stock glanced off the pony's nose, and the animal veered. The brave plunged from his seat and rolled in the boiling dust. Otis jerked the lance from his leg and skewered the Comanche, driving the point through his middle and into the ground. The Indian croaked, twitched and was dead.

The Indian encampment had the appearance of a slaughterhouse, the ground splashed with blood, the area between riddled tipis littered with the dead soldiers, warriors and scores of squaws caught in vicious crossfire. Still, Leaping Wolf's followers fought on. Muzzle flames and smoke puffs burst from clumps of mesquite and pinoaks. Occasionally, a trooper circling on horseback was shot from the saddle.

The war leader himself was no longer to be seen. Marcus Cavanaugh reined up momentarily and searched for Leaping Wolf, but failed to find him. Then, down a slope on his right, a wild howling broke out and the thunder of many hooves. The remaining bulk of Comanche fighting men had grouped for a charge. They tore down on the weakened flank of the soldiers' main force in a densely massed bunch.

Keogh mounted a dead trooper's horse and galloped close to Marcus. "Back off, Major! For God's sake, back off! Here the red devils come!"

"Turn away, hell! If we break this last charge, they're whipped!" Marcus pumped his arm and the troopers rallied. "At 'em men! Give 'em hell!" Marcus flourished his pistol and sped off in the lead. Unless he missed his guess, it was Leaping Wolf riding toward him on a big pony.

The warrior leader's horsemanship was superb. He commenced firing with a shiny, new Winchester, and a trooper near the major toppled. From out of nowhere, a fleet bay dashed past Cavanaugh with dazzling speed, with Nate Ambrose in the saddle, urging his steed with loud shouts. The lieutenant meant to close with the hostiles first. The damned fool was bent on vengeance for the Cantrell woman, but there was nothing Marcus could do to stop him. As the major watched, Ambrose closed with Leaping Wolf and discharged his service Colt. A bloodstain appeared on the warrior chief's arm, a slight wound at best.

The riders passed. Leaping Wolf fired his rifle. Nathan Ambrose's face dissolved in a smear of gore. His body flipped from the saddle, but one foot was caught in a stirrup. The raglike form was dragged by the racing horse and his head was smashed against a rock.

Both charges met at the center of the camp. Troopers and Comanches shot, hacked and flailed at each other. This time Marcus was in the thick of things, shooting a warrior before he could use his hatchet, ramming a pony with Champion, forcing the smaller animal to throw its rider off. He felt a sting in his leg. He'd taken a bullet through his trouser stripe — merely a graze — and rode onward. To his front and sides, Indians and troopers shrieked and plunged from horses' backs. Corporal Malthus and Sergeant Keogh dismounted and fought on the ground.

Major Cavanaugh's powerful mount took a bullet through the neck. Champion went down, gouting draughts of blood. It crumpled in a heap, throwing Marcus clear. Cavanaugh staggered to his feet, dazed. The Colt he'd held was gone, and he looked for it. He saw a soldier's skull being split by an Indian's Bowie knife. The warrior yelped in triumph and ran away.

On the other side of the major, Keogh and a savage dueled ferociously. The sergeant used his empty sidearm against a Spanish saber. The redskin was good with the Toledo blade. One swipe hacked Keogh's Colt from his hand and took a finger off, too. Keogh, bleeding like a stuck pig, dove to wrestle the brave but his knee buckled and he went down.

The brave danced close, aimed a two-handed swing and buried cold steel inches into the sergeant's thigh. Keogh's scream was piercing. Marcus scooped up a Comanche's dropped Dragoon cap-and-ball, and killed Keogh's butcher. In the same moment, he heard unshod hooves pounding up behind him. He spun and confronted Leaping Wolf.

The Comanche war leader flailed with his studded war club as his pony swept near, and missed Marcus narrowly. The major grabbed for his leg, caught it and yanked. The warrior was pulled from the mount. He hit the dirt and rolled. Bounding up, the burly war leader flung himself at Marcus.

The ancient pistol that the major clutched clicked on an empty chamber. He flung it at the warrior's wide chest. The wound inflicted by Nate Ambrose hadn't slowed the war leader. His club now lost, Leaping Wolf pulled his knife, dodged in and slashed with the weapon. Marcus fell back and nearly tripped on a dead Comanche — and the fallen saber. He crouched and scooped up the saber, his fingers closing comfortably on the haft.

He parried the Comanche's next thrust skillfully, and thrust in his turn. The saber's point punctured Leaping Wolf just below his Adam's apple. Bright blood burst from his slit arteries. He toppled and died, his face grimacing in defeat as the last shreds of life left his body. Marcus's shoulders slumped, the saber in his hand suddenly feeling as heavy as a dozen anvils. The frantic sounds of battle died around him, replaced by the moans of the wounded and the wailing of squaws. Turnbo was at his side.

"The redskins are on the run, Major. We've licked them. With their chief dead, they've no more heart for fighting."

"Round up as many survivors as possible. They're bound for the reservation as of this day. The Comanche threat is over in these parts. That should satisfy the generals."

A trooper whooped above the wails of grieving squaws. "Praise be to glory!"

From a nearby tipi, a female voice ventured timidly. "Glory? Th-they used to call m-me Glory!" She threw the flap back and stepped out.

"A blue-eyed girl?" Turnbo exclaimed. "With brown hair?"

"I'm Gloriana Hollister from up Kansas way!" She stepped forward, trembling with fear, as if she did not yet believe that her trials were over.

Marcus reached out to steady the young woman. "Texas has had an ordeal, miss," Major Cavanaugh said firmly, managing his first grin in weeks. "And so have you. But the Comanche threat is over now." His hand closed around hers. For all the brave soldiers and emigrants who were dead — Retta, Virginia and the Chandlers among them — God in His great wisdom had seen fit to restore one tormented woman's freedom. "We've finally made this country safe for folks like you."

When one of his officers disobeys orders and leads the troops into a Sioux ambush, it's up to Colonel Marcus Cavanaugh to rout the savages and avenge . . .

THE TEMPLETON MASSACRE